DETROIT PUBLIC LIBRARY

⟨ **W9-CAD-840**

DETROIT PUBLIC LIBRARY

Browsing Library

DATE DUE

OCT – 9 1996

OCT 1 8 1996

NOV 1 3 1996

DEC – 7 1996

JAN – 2 1997

FEB – 1 1997

BC-3

SEP 2 1 1996

Death Au Gratin

By the same author:

THE SPIRAL PATH
MADMAN'S WHISPER
DEATH IN MELTING
DEAD SO SOON
MURDER RED HANDED
SPY IN CAMERA
PLAY THE ROMAN FOOL AND DIE
A TASTE OF DEATH
THE MURDERS AT IMPASSE LOUVAIN
THE MONTERANT AFFAIR
THE DEATH OF ABBE DIDIER
THE MONTMARTRE MURDERS
DEATH STALK
CRIME WITHOUT PASSION
THE WHISKY MURDERS
DEATH EN VOYAGE
DEATH ON THE CARDS
DEATH OFF STAGE

as Richard Grindal

OVER THE SEA TO DIE
THE TARTAN CONSPIRACY

Death Au Gratin

Richard Grayson

St. Martin's Press
New York

M

DEATH AU GRATIN. Copyright © 1994 by Richard Grayson. All rights reserved. Printed in the United States of America. No part of this book may be used or reproduced in any manner whatsoever without written permission except in the case of brief quotations embodied in critical articles or reviews. For information, address St. Martin's Press, 175 Fifth Avenue, New York, N.Y. 10010.

Library of Congress Cataloging-in-Publication Data

Grayson, Richard.
    Death au gratin / Richard Grayson.
      p. cm.
    ISBN 0-312-13047-3
    1. Gautier, Jean-Paul (Fictitious character)—Fiction.
    2. Police—France—Paris—Fiction.   3. Paris (France)—Fiction.
    I. Title.
    PR6057.R55D378   1995
    823'.914—dc20   95-14720
                                                        CIP

First published in Great Britain by Macmillan London Limited

First U.S. Edition: August 1995
10 9 8 7 6 5 4 3 2 1

BL AFX9303
SEP 2 1 1996

Chapter 1

'Eh, Windsor! Are you buying the champagne?' Le Coussin called out loudly.

She had just finished her dance, ending with a flourish by raising her skirts to show the hearts embroidered on her frilly pants and two or three inches of generous thigh. She seemed to hold the pose for a shade longer than usual, thrusting her hips suggestively towards the portly, bearded man in evening dress, who was sitting at a nearby table with two companions. The audience, many of whom were *habitués* of the Moulin Rouge and may have recognized the portly man, began laughing and clapping.

Monsieur Windsor laughed too and seemed delighted. 'Only if Mademoiselle does me the honour of joining us,' he called back.

Le Coussin went to his table and he rose, kissed her hand and held the chair which a waiter had brought up for her. His companions too kissed the dancer's hand. Champagne was brought and poured for them as one of the others of the troupe began to perform. The Moulin Rouge's dancers, many of them enticed away from a rival establishment, the Elysée Montmartre, were its principal attraction. Le Coussin was the star, but most of the others were known throughout Paris, also by their nicknames: Cri-Cri la Grimace, La Sauterelle, Lili Jambe-en-L'air and Zagoda the belly dancer, who performed on the stage in the garden alongside its huge stuffed elephant.

'Anyone might think that it was she who was the royalty,' Claire Ryan said to Gautier.

Gautier smiled and placed one finger over Claire's lips.

1

Monsieur Windsor was visiting Paris incognito and the dancers and staff of the Moulin Rouge had been warned to be discreet. Gautier supposed that he and Claire Ryan should put on a show of discretion as well, particularly as he was officially there on duty that evening, watching to see that Monsieur Windsor came to no harm.

A few weeks previously he had been given a special assignment as part of his duties as a chief inspector of the Sûreté. Ever since France, afraid of being left isolated and without allies in Europe, had entered into the Entente Cordiale with Britain, the French Government had been most solicitous for the safety of any English who came to Paris. Courtrand, the Director General of the Sûreté, had instructed Gautier to arrange that any important visitors – royalty, milords and politicians – be kept under a discreet surveillance, so that they could be given protection if they should need it. Policemen would be posted near the entrances of the hotels in which they were staying, and other officers in plain clothes would follow them if they went out to restaurants or theatres or to sample what they believed were the naughty pleasures of Paris by night, in cabarets, dance-halls and bordellos.

Courtrand, who was jealous of Gautier as easily the youngest of the Sûreté's inspectors and of his frequent successes in solving spectacular crimes, usually gave him the most boring and tiresome assignments. This one, though, Gautier had turned to his advantage. His knowledge of English was rudimentary, restricted to a few words of courtesy, so he had obtained permission to take lessons in the language and had been taking them from Claire Ryan.

Claire was Irish, the illegitimate daughter of an earl, who was living at that time in Paris. Gautier had met her when he was investigating the murders of a judge and a ballet dancer. They had become lovers, and the excuse of English lessons allowed them to meet alone and more often than social conventions would normally allow.

'That was rather a cheeky remark for that dancer to make, was it not?' Claire asked him.

'She calculated that our English friend would not mind. They say he will forgive a pretty girl almost anything.'

'Yes, I've heard he has earned that reputation in Paris,' Claire said, and then she added, 'Do you find her pretty?'

'Le Coussin? Not pretty, but she has a way with her that one.' Gautier had been tempted to say that Le Coussin was pretty in a vulgar sort of way, but he thought it might sound patronizing, even though the chief asset of the principal dancer at the Moulin Rouge was her vulgarity. She had made herself popular among the clientele of the Moulin largely by imitating the manners and the style of her predecessor, La Goulue. A decade ago, it had been La Goulue who had first attracted crowds to the dance-hall when it had not long been opened. With her plump, pink face, her blonde hair cut in a fringe above her eyebrows, a chignon on top of her head and her abundant bosom freely escaping from her corsage, Le Coussin looked very like La Goulue and had been quick to exploit the resemblance.

'The cushion; a strange nickname for a dancer,' Claire remarked. 'I suppose I need not ask the reason for it.'

'No. She will have provided comfort for a good many men.'

'Are all the dancers here – ' Claire hesitated over a choice of expression. She had been well brought up by her father the earl, notwithstanding the circumstances of her birth.

'Not all of them supplement their income after the performance is over.' Gautier smiled as he helped her out of her difficulty. 'Though they were obliged to when the Moulin first opened.'

He told Claire how Ziddler, a butcher turned impresario, had bought La Reine Blanche, an undistinguished *guinguette* in Boulevard de Clichy, below the Butte of Montmartre. Ziddler had pulled the place down and built the Moulin Rouge, crowning its entrance with a giant mock windmill with bright red sails which could be made to turn. The existing cabarets and *guinguettes* around Montmartre had been mainly patronized by young work-

3

men, with a leavening of prostitutes, pimps, thieves and cut-throats. Within a few years, Ziddler was drawing a different clientele from the bourgeoisie. They were soon followed by visitors from abroad: the English, the Russians and wealthy Americans off transatlantic liners, attracted by the *risqué* vulgarity of the *quartier*. The upper crust of French society, the *gratin* as it was called, would never condone a visit to the Moulin Rouge, but Monsieur Windsor frequently disregarded the conventions of society in France as well as in England.

At first, Ziddler did not pay his dancers. Now the Moulin Rouge was becoming a legend and Le Coussin was supposed to be earning one thousand francs a month, at a time when little seamstresses were paid two francs a day.

'I'm so glad you brought me here,' Claire said, 'I would not have missed it for the world.'

What attracted Gautier about Claire, apart from her red hair, pale, freckled skin and – he had to admit – her body, was her love of life. She approached every new experience, including some they had shared in bed, with an almost innocent naivety and eagerness. She was also generous in showing her appreciation.

'How amazed my friends back home will be when I tell them,' she added.

'It might be wiser not to tell them everything you have done in Paris,' Gautier teased her gently.

'Why should I not? We have nothing to be ashamed of!' she answered defiantly, but Gautier could see a sadness in her eyes as she reached out and placed a hand on his.

The Moulin Rouge did not offer entertainment suitable for young ladies of careful upbringing, but Claire had begged Gautier to take her there, and he had agreed because it was her last night in Paris. The following day she would travel back to Ireland to live with her father's sister. She was still young enough for the Earl to have hopes that they might yet find a husband for her.

Gautier was sad too, but he would not give in to sadness and spoil her last evening. Later, when they were alone, there would be time for them to share their melancholy.

4

So he tried to raise her spirits by telling her some of the stories about the dancers at the Moulin Rouge which were causing hilarity among Parisians.

As the evening passed, the music and the laughter grew noisier, the dancing more vigorous and daring. Monsieur Windsor appeared to be enjoying himself, but was paying more attention to Le Coussin than to the performance on the stage. Soon it would be time for the *Quadrille Naturaliste*, a dance performed by eight dancers, which dated back to the Second Empire and which was becoming internationally famous under the name of the cancan.

Shortly before it was due to begin, Gautier heard raised voices and saw that there was a disturbance by the entrance to the hall. The two doormen, who had been reinforced that evening by a policeman from the local *commissariat*, were restraining a man who was shouting at them. Quickly excusing himself, Gautier left their table and crossed the hall towards them. He had been half expecting something like this.

The man who was creating the disturbance did not look like a drunk or a *voyou* from Montmartre. He wore evening dress, with a monocle hanging from his buttonhole, and must also have been carrying a top-hat, for one lay on the floor behind him, knocked there no doubt as he struggled to free himself from the grip of the doormen.

'You have no right to stop me coming in,' he shouted at them.

'I regret, Monsieur, that we do. The law gives us the right to exclude anyone who might cause trouble.'

'I am not here to make trouble. All I wish is to speak with that gentleman over there.' The man pointed in the direction of Monsieur Windsor.

'That will not be possible, Monsieur. You must leave.'

At this the man shouted again, still pointing towards Monsieur Windsor, 'Adulterer! Libertine!'

'Take the gentleman outside,' Gautier told the two doormen.

'Who are you?' the man demanded. 'On what authority do you give orders?'

'This is Chief Inspector Gautier of the Sûreté,' the

5

policeman told him. Gautier was known to most of the local police officers in the *arrondissements* of Paris.

The doormen began leading the man out of the hall. Perhaps because now the Sûreté was involved, the man did not resist, but in a final show of defiance he shouted abuse at Monsieur Windsor over his shoulder.

'How did you come here this evening?' Gautier asked him when they were outside.

'In my automobile of course.' The man pointed at a De Dion-Bouton which stood in the street, its chauffeur waiting at the wheel.

'Then have your chauffeur drive you home. If you return or try to embarrass our English visitor in any other way this evening, you will be arrested and spend the night in jail,' Gautier said, and he watched as the man reluctantly obeyed him.

Inside the Moulin Rouge, the cancan had begun. Most of the audience had not been aware of the incident that had taken place near the entrance. If any of them had heard the man's shouts of abuse, they would probably not have known at whom they were directed.

'What was all that?' Claire asked Gautier when he sat down beside her.

'A rather ineffectual attempt to embarrass our English guest and cause a scandal.'

'Who was that man?'

'The Comte de Chartres.'

'What is his grudge against Monsieur Windsor?'

Gautier told Claire that the Comte Edmond de Chartres was one of the less distinguished relics of the French aristocracy that had survived the purge of the Revolution. He was married to the daughter of an immensely wealthy Spanish grandee, and seven or eight years ago his wife had for a time been the mistress of Monsieur Windsor, sleeping with him during his not infrequent visits to Paris.

'Are you saying that this happened all that time ago, but the Comte has only just found out?'

'Unfortunately, a *cocu* is all too often the last to hear of his wife's infidelity.'

Gautier spoke from experience. Some years previously, when his wife went to live with a policeman from the 15th *Arrondissement*, he had only learnt of her infidelity after she had left their home.

'And the Comte came here this evening just to shout abuse at Monsieur Windsor? As revenge, that would not be very satisfying, I would have thought.'

'I believe he had something more in mind. He had white gloves with his evening dress, as one would expect, but was wearing only the left-hand glove and carrying the other in his hand. Had he reached Monsieur Windsor, he could have slapped him across the face with the glove.'

'Challenging him to a duel?'

'Exactly.'

Although duelling was supposed to be against the law in France, gentlemen not infrequently met at dawn to settle their differences with the épée or pistols. Usually these confrontations in the Bois de Boulogne ended with, at the most, a trifling flesh wound, but honour was felt to be satisfied.

'Surely Monsieur Windsor would not be allowed to fight him?'

'Of course not, and in any case he is leaving Paris tomorrow. But the Comte de Chartres could claim a sort of satisfaction, and no doubt the challenge would be reported in the newspapers. He would see to that.'

'You say that Monsieur Windsor is returning to England tomorrow? Do you think he may be travelling on the same train as I?'

'I understand that they travel on a special train on these occasions.'

Gautier was not certain that what he said was true, but he did not want Claire to have any false hopes. He sensed that any sadness she felt at leaving Paris and leaving him was being overtaken by the excitement of the journey ahead and seeing her home and her Irish friends again. Any disappointment she may have felt at learning that she would not be travelling with royalty did not last long, for as they were talking, one of Monsieur Windsor's companions came over to their table. Gautier knew that his name was Forbes and that he was either Monsieur Windsor's secretary or equerry. He was not sure which, because, like most Frenchmen, he was baffled by the subtle distinctions of protocol at the English court. It had been Forbes who, throughout their visit to Paris, had kept Gautier informed every day of Monsieur Windsor's movements.

'I have been asked to give you this, Monsieur,' he said, handing Gautier a visiting card. On one side of the card, Monsieur Windsor's name was printed without any address, and on the other, a brief note had been written in English. It read:

Monsieur, we are greatly obliged to you for your timely and tactful intervention. Please accept this small token of our gratitude. W.

As he read it, Gautier noticed that Forbes had been followed to their table by a waiter carrying a bottle of champagne and two glasses on a tray. He told Forbes, 'Please be so kind as to thank Monsieur Windsor and tell him that I am always at his disposition.'

'Willingly,' Forbes replied. He spoke excellent French. Then he smiled as he added, 'You may be relieved to hear, Monsieur Gautier, that we are going home directly from here.'

'To the home of Madame Brandon?'

'Yes. Her carriage is already here to take us there.' Forbes glanced at Claire and smiled mischievously as he added, 'So you may end your vigil and go home too.'

Mrs Laura Brandon was a wealthy English widow who had made her home in Paris. On his incognito visits, Monsieur Windsor invariably stayed at her home in Avenue du Bois de Boulogne. People said she had been his mistress when they were both much younger. Now she was one of the leading hostesses in Paris and, whatever her past, her reputation was inviolable.

Gautier was pleased to hear that Monsieur Windsor

had decided to end his evening of entertainment. On other occasions he had been known to carry on into the early hours of the morning, sometimes visiting exclusive houses in Rue de Richelieu where expensive pleasures were available. Had he done so that evening, Gautier would have been obliged to continue his discreet watch, and he could hardly have taken Claire with him. And that would have meant that he and Claire could not have shared her last evening in Paris in the way he had hoped they might.

After Forbes had left them, he noticed that Claire was looking at the note which Monsieur Windsor had sent him and he could sense her curiosity. There was enough room at the top of the card for him to write a brief note on it.

Claire. A little memento of the evening we spent at the Moulin Rouge. Jean-Paul.

When he handed the card to Claire, she was delighted. Gautier knew that she had been collecting souvenirs of her stay in Paris to take back to Ireland. She had showed him some of them: the programme of a performance of *Le Spectre du Nil* by the Dashkova Russian ballet company, a hand-painted fan presented to ladies who had helped at a charity fête, a copy of a new volume of verse by Renée de Saules signed by the poetess, a small brass model of the Eiffel Tower. A handwritten note from royalty would really crown her collection.

'You're so good to me, Jean-Paul. How can I repay all your kindnesses?'

'You already have.'

Claire smiled and once again reached out to touch his hand. 'We still have some time left together.'

They drank the champagne and watched as Monsieur Windsor and his companions left. Soon afterwards, a uniformed police officer came to their table. Gautier recognized him as one of two men who had been on duty at the Hôtel Meurice. The Meurice was popular with English visitors, many of whom stayed there when they came to Paris for the races at Longchamps. Gautier had arranged for two men to be on duty outside the hotel that evening because another important Englishman, Sigmund Locke, was staying there that week. Locke was a banker, a partner in the firm of Locke and Locke, which had done great service to France by lending the country part of the money needed to pay off the massive indemnity demanded after her defeat by Germany in 1871. As the policeman was approaching, Gautier had a presentiment that the news he was bringing would be unwelcome.

'Chief Inspector,' the man said, 'I thought you should know that a woman has been found dead in the Hôtel Meurice.'

'An English woman?'

'No, Monsieur. One of the hotel chambermaids.'

'How did she die? Was it an accident?'

'No. She was bitten by a poisonous snake.'

Chapter 2

In spite of its reputation for elegance, its colonnades and the Jardin des Tuileries, Gautier had always found Rue de Rivoli a gloomy street. Late at night it was even more depressing. As one left Place de la Concorde and passed the austere buildings of the Palais Royal, the elegance was soon supplanted and the street became a long finger pointing reproachfully at Place de la Bastille. That night the street was silent and so was the Hôtel Meurice, its lobby and staircases empty. Gautier could not sense any of the excitement and fear that sudden death usually provoked.

The chambermaid's body, covered with a blanket, still lay on the floor of the bedroom in which she had died. The corpse of the snake, its head severed from its long, scaly body, lay on the carpet some distance away. The head was unlike that of any snake Gautier had seen before. The only other people in the room were the manager of the hotel, who had been called out from his bed, and a doctor who had arrived only a short time ago. Doctors were hard to find in Paris after midnight. This one at least seemed to have finished his examination of the maid's body.

'Tell me what happened,' Gautier said to the manager.

'We do not know exactly. One of the other chambermaids found her in convulsions on the floor. When she saw the snake, her screams brought other members of the staff running. But poor Yvette died before we could do anything for her.'

'Who killed the snake?'

11

'The sous chef on duty. He slashed the beast with a sword which he took off the wall in the drawing-room.'

'A brave man!' the doctor remarked. 'He could have been bitten as well.'

'At what hour did it happen?'

'We do not know. Some hours ago perhaps, for she did not die at once. It would seem that she came in to turn the bed down as she always did, for as you can see the bedcover and top blanket have been pulled down. The snake may have been in the bed.'

'Very possibly it came in here in darkness,' the doctor suggested. 'They hunt at night for rats.'

'There are no rats in my hotel,' the manager said indignantly.

'What species of snake is it?' Gautier asked.

'A cobra,' the doctor replied. '*Naja naja* they call it in India.'

'You are very well informed.'

'I served as a doctor in the merchant marine for a time. When our ship put in at Bombay, snake charmers would be performing on the quay.'

'Am I right in believing that the cobra is not indigenous to France?'

'Yes. One finds them only in tropical and semi-tropical countries.'

'Then how has one arrived in my hotel?' The manager was becoming increasingly anxious, wondering no doubt whether there might be snakes in other rooms.

'It may have escaped from captivity,' the doctor suggested. 'There is a reptile house in that private zoo in Passy.'

A much more plausible explanation, Gautier decided, was that the cobra had been brought into the hotel and released into the bed. Then when the chambermaid turned down the bedcover and blankets it came out and bit her.

'Who is occupying this bedroom, Monsieur?' he asked the manager.

'Monsieur Armand de Périgord,' the manager replied.

Then he understood the implication of Gautier's question. 'What are you suggesting, Inspector? That the snake was put in the bed deliberately to attack Monsieur de Périgord, to kill him? It's inconceivable! An outrageous suggestion!'

'Where is Monsieur de Périgord?'

'Out for the evening, one supposes. Dining with friends, no doubt. He seldom spends the evening here.'

'For how long has he been staying with you?'

The manager seemed surprised at the question. 'Did you not know that Monsieur de Périgord lives in the hotel permanently? This suite, the best in the Hôtel Meurice, is always occupied by him, except of course when he goes to stay at his château in the country.'

Gautier had met Monsieur de Périgord once briefly on a social occasion and he knew him better, as many people did, by his reputation. Armand Frédéric de Périgord was one of those characters who from time to time surface in a social milieu to which they do not belong but in which they are quickly assimilated. In spite of a provincial upbringing, he had all the qualities needed as an entrée to the upper echelons of Paris society: culture, good manners and wealth. Since he was not known to work for a living, people assumed that the wealth was inherited, and no one really knew from where it came, although the jealous hinted that his grandfather had amassed it by dubious means in the shady parts of Marseilles. As he was unmarried and rich, he was much in demand as a guest at dinner parties and on other social occasions. Also, as he was unmarried and over forty, people assumed that he must be homosexual.

'If you gentlemen have no further need of my services,' the doctor said, 'may I leave?'

'By all means. Thank you for your assistance.'

'You will have my report tomorrow and, in the meantime, I shall arrange for the young woman's body to be taken away to the mortuary.'

'I will leave you too, Inspector,' the hotel manager said, 'at least for a short time. I must arrange for another bedroom to be put at Monsieur de Périgord's disposal. We cannot expect him to sleep here after what has happened.'

'Would you also be kind enough to arrange for the head and body of the snake to be wrapped up and put in safe keeping? We may need it for scientific examination. And one thing more. I would like a list of all the guests staying here tonight. Please have one made for me and I will have it collected tomorrow morning.'

After the two men had left, Gautier looked round the suite, which was the finest in the hotel with its rooms overlooking Rue de Rivoli and the Jardin des Tuileries beyond. Both the drawing-room and the bedroom were enormous, and the suite had a bathroom, a rare luxury as it was only within the last few years that bathrooms were being constructed, even in private houses and apartments. Those Parisians who took a bath did so in tin baths filled with jugs of hot water by their servants.

Gautier found nothing in the suite which would explain why or how a poisonous snake had been brought in there, nor had he expected that he would. All three rooms, however, reflected the character and habits of the man who was occupying them. The wardrobe in the bedroom was full of well-tailored suits and more linen than a working man might come to possess in a lifetime. In the privacy of the bathroom were rows of bottles and sachets, lotions for the skin and hair made up by pharmacists, brilliantine, dyes and stains, all designed to project at least the outward appearance of youth.

On a table in the drawing-room lay a catholic selection of books, some with their pages still uncut, slim volumes of poetry by the young literati of the *quartier latin*, scholarly works by members of the Académie française and the erotic novels of Rachilde and Colette. Next to the books were two photographs, both in silver frames. One of the photographs was of an elderly lady in a black dress and a toque hat. The other was of de Périgord, posing with a man older than himself who Gautier thought might be Oscar Wilde. In the centre of the room stood an easel supporting an unframed painting of a young woman with a swan neck and oval face, which Gautier decided must

14

be the work of one of the band of new young artists now living in Montmartre, Modigliani perhaps.

The paintings in the room, he supposed, would be the property of the hotel, but hanging on one wall was a collection of swords, artistically arranged, three in their scabbards and two bare blades with ornate, engraved hilts. There was a space in the collection, presumably for the sword which had been snatched off the wall and used to kill the snake.

On the writing desk in the room were a silver inkwell and a quill pen, but neither gave the impression that they were often used. Gautier noticed the corner of a scrap of paper sticking out from one of the desk's drawers which had been only partially closed. Pulling the paper out he saw that it was a cutting from a newspaper of a regular feature which gave the appointments and movements of the diplomatic corps. The item which had been cut out reported that France's Ambassador to the Court of St James had that day returned to London after a short visit to Paris for consultations. The cutting did not carry a date.

Gautier had time to no more than glance at it and put it back in the drawer when he heard the door to the corridor open and the hotel manager came in accompanied by Armand de Périgord. De Périgord was a tall man, not unhandsome, whose complexion and colouring suggested that he might come from the Midi. He had the figure of an athlete, but something in his manner and posture hinted that behind the façade of masculinity lay a delicacy and fastidiousness more often found in women.

'This is Monsieur de Périgord, Inspector,' the manager introduced them, and de Périgord inclined his head in the smallest bow that one could imagine.

'Have you been told of the death of the chambermaid in your bedroom?' Gautier asked de Périgord.

'I have, and, as I have already remarked, it is inconceivable that such a thing should have been allowed in a hotel of standing.'

'We shall discover how it happened in due course, no doubt.'

'I should hope so. You will appreciate that this means someone is trying to kill me?'

'Not necessarily, Monsieur. Whoever placed the snake in the bed may well have known that it was the chambermaid who would turn down the bed.'

'Who would wish to kill a chambermaid?'

Gautier shrugged. 'A jealous colleague perhaps. If it comes to that, who would wish to kill you?'

'All men have enemies and I have more than most.'

'Is it not possible,' the manager suggested, 'that the attack was meant for another guest in the hotel. An English banker has a suite on this floor.'

Gautier recognized the implication of the suggestion. A chauvinist like most Frenchmen, the manager would prefer it that an incident so potentially damaging to his hotel could be blamed on foreigners.

'Impossible!' de Périgord said. 'People don't murder bankers. No, there can be no doubt that the snake was intended to kill me. *Merde* to them! My enemies will discover that I am not one to be eliminated so easily!'

Was this the contempt of fear that brave men were supposed to feel, Gautier found himself wondering, or just bravado? He could see a glaze across de Périgord's eyes, which suggested that he had been drinking, and it might be better if alcohol had dulled his senses, for then he might sleep more easily.

Aware that there was nothing more he could do that night, Gautier left the two men together, de Périgord still noisily truculent, the manager solicitous for his guest and for his hotel's reputation. In the morning, he would have to put in train a more rigorous investigation. He was confident that it would not be difficult to trace the source from which the snake had come. There would be few cobras in Paris, but he could think of other questions the answers to which might be more revealing.

The hotel lobby was deserted except for Henri, the night porter, who was sitting in a chair behind the concierge's desk. Gautier went to have a word with him. Henri was a former policeman who had left the force of the 7th

16

Arrondissement to become a hotel porter. No one knew why he had decided to accept this loss of status.

'That was a terrible business here tonight, Inspector,' Henri said after the two men had shaken hands.

'Most regrettable.'

'Poor little Yvette! Such a sweet girl! So kind and helpful! Always ready to do a colleague a good turn.'

'You don't think the snake was put in the room to kill her?'

'Never! Everyone loved Yvette.'

'How do you suppose the snake was brought into the hotel? One could not carry a snake in one's hands. So it must have been hidden; in a valise, or perhaps a box.'

'I have been thinking about that.' Henri looked worried. 'Do you think I shall be blamed for allowing it to be brought in?'

Gautier tried to reassure him. In his opinion, the snake would not have been brought in at night, but earlier in the evening or afternoon when the arrival of a package would be less likely to be noticed.

'Do you suppose that the Englishman could be involved in this?' Henri asked.

'Monsieur Locke? What makes you think he might be?'

'This is the first time that he and his wife have stayed with us. They often come to Paris, but until this time they have always stayed at the Ritz.'

Gautier could think of many reasons why Sigmund Locke should have decided to try a different hotel, but he did not say so. The porter must have some reason, other than xenophobia, for believing that Locke might be involved in the incident of the cobra and he wanted to find out what that was.

'Has the Englishman been a difficult guest?' he asked Henri.

'Not at all. He's very courteous to the staff and tips well.' Henri hesitated before he continued, 'His wife is much younger than he is, you understand, and very beautiful.'

This, Gautier thought, was going to be a new twist to

17

the expression '*cherchez la femme*', but he did not laugh. With a little encouragement, Henri might explain the tortuous logic behind his suspicions. He did. A few nights previously, he told Gautier, he had been summoned very late at night to the room on the third floor of another guest, who was complaining that he could not open the windows. That was the way of the English with their absurd passion for fresh air. As he was coming downstairs again, Henri had noticed someone moving in the first-floor corridor and saw that it was a woman. She was wearing a dressing-gown and moving stealthily, so he had stopped to watch her.

'I saw then that it was Madame Locke,' he told Gautier. 'She went along the corridor and into Monsieur de Périgord's suite.'

'Are you certain of that?'

'Absolutely. She did not knock on the door but went straight in, so it could not have been locked on the inside. I waited for some minutes, but she did not come out.'

'Have you told anyone of this?'

'Only one person. I mentioned it to Yvette.'

'And what did she say?'

'She did not seem surprised. It seems that more than once when she made Monsieur de Périgord's bed, she had noticed the smell of a woman's perfume on the sheets.'

Gautier did not wish to give the impression that he doubted the porter, nor that he was accepting his story too readily. So he said, 'You should not have left the police, old fellow. You would make a good detective. But it would be wiser if for the present you did not tell anyone else what you saw.'

'I won't, Inspector. You can rely on that.'

Outside the hotel, Gautier found a fiacre whose driver agreed, after a good deal of grumbling, to drive him to his apartment. The drivers of fiacres were an independent breed, apt to refuse fares which would take them too far from their own *quartier* late at night, and this one seemed to have an aversion to the Left Bank. As they drove towards the Seine, Gautier remembered how he had hoped this evening with Claire would end. Had he not

18

been called to the Hôtel Meurice, they would have gone from the Moulin Rouge to another luxury hotel where a room was being kept for them. Over the past weeks, whenever they had made love it had been at the same hotel, where Gautier was on good terms with the management as a result of a favour he had done them in the past. He had flinched from taking a girl of Claire's upbringing to one of the many *hôtels-de-rendezvous* in Paris, and had always thought it would not be proper to take her to his apartment. It was an old-fashioned idea, he supposed, but that was how he felt.

So when they had left the Moulin Rouge, he had put Claire in a fiacre and told the driver to take her to the Earl of Newry's apartment in Parc Monceau. She would be leaving Paris the following afternoon, and he might meet her once more, but only briefly, if his duties allowed him to see her off at the Gare du Nord.

He would miss Claire, not only for their love-making, but for her companionship. There had been other women in his life since Suzanne had left him. He remembered them all, some for the intensity of their passion, some with affection for their kindness. In retrospect, none of them, though, had possessed Claire's very individual charm, a combination of innocence, vitality and unfailing good nature. As wearily he climbed the three flights of stairs to his apartment, he was aware that he must not indulge in a sentiment which could easily become maudlin.

When he reached the apartment and saw a light shining under the door, memory played a trick on him and he wondered for an instant if Suzanne had come back to him. But Suzanne was dead, dying a year or two after she had left him, giving birth to the child which Gaston, her lover, had fathered. He supposed then that the woman who came in to clean the apartment for him each morning must have forgotten to turn off the gas lamps.

His assumption seemed to be borne out when he found no one in the living-room of the apartment. Then he saw that a light was shining in his bedroom as well, and he heard Claire's voice call, 'I'm in here.'

Chapter 3

Sitting in his office at Sûreté headquarters next morning, Gautier remembered the hours that had followed his return home. He did not usually allow himself the luxury of day-dreaming at his desk, but he had already written a report on the incident at the Moulin Rouge and another on the death in the Hôtel Meurice and taken them to the office of Courtrand, the Director General, on the floor above his. Courtrand worked gentlemen's hours and was not likely to be arriving for an hour or more.

When he had gone into his bedroom he had seen Claire lying in his bed. She was covered by a sheet but he knew she was naked. It had brought back memories, for the first time they had made love she had insisted on going into the bedroom before him and that was how he had found her. Even though she had never had a man before, she had not been bashful. He had soon learned that she was proud of her body and eager to make love, and that was how it had remained throughout their brief liaison.

Last night there had been all kinds of questions he wished to ask her. How had she known where he lived? How did she get into the apartment? What would her father, the Earl, think if she stayed out all night? Gautier had never kept her out so late before. The questions had remained unanswered, his curiosity and his anxiety stifled by her passion. He recalled her telling him once that all she knew about sex she had learned from reading second-hand books on the bookstalls beside the Seine. Now, after only a few weeks, she knew things about love-making which no books could have taught her. Last night she had

20

been the imperious partner, the caresses of her fingers and her lips kindling an ecstasy almost too intense to be endured. Then finally, at first light, when she knew she must leave him, she kissed him fiercely.

'There! Now you'll never forget me!'

Recognizing that memories of the previous night and thoughts of Claire could end in self-pity, he put them from his mind. Work had to be planned, investigations arranged. He sent for Surat, his principal assistant, and let him read a copy of the report he had written on the death of the chambermaid Yvette.

'First of all, we need to find out where that snake came from,' he told him when he had finished reading. Then, because he liked to encourage Surat to use his initiative, he asked him, 'Have you any ideas?'

'At the Alcazar music-hall, one of the turns is a girl who, I understand, dances covered only in snakes.'

'They would hardly be poisonous snakes.'

'I suppose not. What about some of those small fairs one finds in the *quartiers*? The other day I saw one which had performing bears and monkeys.'

Surat was a conscientious policeman, courageous and loyal, especially to Gautier, but he had always been passed over for promotion, and Gautier could understand why. In the end, though, the solving of crimes always needed hard work, routine and unimaginative, and he knew of no one who did that better than Surat.

'I suggest we start at the Sorbonne,' he said. 'Professor Léon in the department of natural sciences is an authority on reptiles. He would know if there are any cobras in the zoos and menageries of Paris. They may even have some at the university for scientific purposes. Go and show him the remains of the snake. You'll find him very helpful.'

'And should we make enquiries at the Hôtel Meurice?'

'Yes. Send two men to question the hotel staff. I would like to know how that snake was smuggled into the hotel, and it may well have been through the staff entrance.'

Gautier knew that at the Meurice, as at all hotels of standing, porters or pages were always hovering at the entrance. Anyone arriving with a valise or basket would immediately be relieved of it, for guests were not supposed to carry anything through the lobbies. That was what the staff were for and, more important, that was how they earned their tips. After Surat had left, he went upstairs to see Corbin, the Director General's secretary. Corbin was a little gnome of a man who worked in a room not much larger than a broom cupboard next to Courtrand's office.

'I suppose you have come to see whether I have a file on Armand de Périgord,' he said to Gautier.

'How did you guess?'

'I have read the report which you put on the Director General's desk.'

Corbin was proud of his secret files. Courtrand's appointment as head of the Sûreté had been a piece of political patronage, a return for services which he had rendered some Government minister in the past. To show his gratitude and, he hoped, to protect his position, he saw to it that a major concern of the Sûreté was the safety and well-being of important people. All possible measures were taken to ensure that Government ministers, politicians, prominent businessmen and members of the aristocracy should not be inconvenienced in any way and, when necessary, that they were given protection.

In order to assist his chief, Corbin had for some years being painstakingly building files on important people. In the file on, for example, the Minister for the Interior, one could find not only detailed information on his education, career and main interests, but the names of his relatives and where they lived and worked. Gautier knew that some files even gave details of any amorous liaisons a man might have enjoyed and of any indiscretions that may have resulted from them.

All such information was kept in buff folders tied with ribbon, and the folders were stored in a cupboard that covered one wall of Corbin's office. When he needed one, he would open the cupboard with a key which he kept chained to his waist. In Gautier's view, Corbin was

22

inclined to have delusions of grandeur about the importance of his files.

'Monsieur de Périgord is scarcely a person of sufficient importance to justify a file,' he told Gautier.

'But you do have one on him?'

'Yes. Not as a person of consequence but more as a potential source of trouble.'

'What kind of trouble?'

Corbin's nose wrinkled with distaste. 'With homosexuals there can always be trouble; blackmail, for example.'

'Do we know that he is a pederast?'

'He was one of the few people who befriended the Englishman, Oscar Wilde, when he came to Paris. There's a note on that in the file.' Corbin glanced at the file. 'And then there was that book of poetry which he published.'

Gautier remembered the book of verses which de Périgord had published some years previously and which had created a stir in Paris society. He had never read them himself but knew that the poems had homosexual themes and that the book had been strongly condemned by the Catholic Church. Corbin handed the file to Gautier, who began reading what it contained, which did not go much beyond bare biographical details. One item did however catch his attention. De Périgord was known to have fought at least two duels. One had ended harmlessly enough, but in the second, his opponent, a Frenchman married to a Brazilian heiress, had been seriously wounded.

'This duel,' Gautier said to Corbin. 'Since we knew that he wounded his opponent, why did de Périgord not have to face charges in court?'

Corbin looked uncomfortable. He would have preferred not to have answered Gautier's question but he was an honest man. 'Shall we say that influential people intervened on his behalf.'

'So he has powerful friends?'

'Not friends, but he once did some work for the Government. Consequently, an important Government department did not want him to be too closely questioned in court.'

Gautier was about to ask Corbin if he might study the file on de Périgord, but before he could, a bell rang in the office. Recently, Courtrand had arranged for electric bells to be fitted in Corbin's office and also in Gautier's, so that he could summon them at will. Courtrand was deeply suspicious of electricity, as he was of telephones, and which he had only reluctantly allowed them to be installed in Sûreté headquarters. Now he used the bell as often as he could to demonstrate his authority. This time Gautier followed Corbin into the Director General's office.

'Ah, there you are, Gautier!' Courtrand said petulantly. 'I've been ringing for you.'

'Monsieur?'

'I am very concerned by your report of the incident at the Moulin Rouge last night. You should have expected that the Comte de Chartres would try to embarrass our royal visitor.'

'We thought he might and so we made sure he would not succeed.'

Courtrand made a disparaging noise to show his scepticism. 'Let us hope we do not receive a complaint from the Ambassador.'

'That's most unlikely. Monsieur Windsor thanked me for the way we handled the affair.'

'He thanked you? Personally?' Courtrand's jealousy flared.

'No. His secretary brought me a note from him,' Gautier replied, and he could not resist adding, 'and a bottle of champagne to show his appreciation.'

'In that case, I hope at least that the cost of the champagne will be deducted from the expenses you will no doubt be claiming for visiting that vulgar establishment. Moulin Rouge, indeed!'

Gautier decided to ignore the remark in spite of its pettiness. So he said, 'Enquiries into the death at the Hôtel Meurice have already been put in hand, Monsieur.'

'What death? Oh, you mean that business of the chambermaid?'

'The hotel management are very concerned.'

'They should blame themselves for allowing a debauchee like de Périgord to live permanently in their establishment. They should expect trouble.'

Obviously, Courtrand took the view that the death of a hotel maid was not of sufficient importance to cause him any concern. Instead, he reminded Gautier that Monsieur Windsor would be leaving Paris for London later that day. 'I shall be at the Gare du Nord to see him leave,' he concluded, 'and to make sure that his safety is not put in jeopardy.'

When Gautier arrived at the Hôtel Meurice, he was told that Armand de Périgord would be willing to receive him in his suite. The bedroom of the suite had a door which opened on to the corridor and when Gautier passed it was slightly open. Inside, decorators were at work, stripping the wallpaper and repainting the woodwork. He was mildly irritated that the hotel should have started the redecorating without first asking him, but he did not believe that a search of the room would have produced any clues to the identity of the person who had taken the snake there. In England, the police made much of fingerprinting, a science which had been discovered in British India not long previously. The Sûreté was also assembling a library of fingerprints, but it was in its infancy and did not yet have enough prints to be of any value in crime detection.

De Périgord was in the drawing-room of the suite and had just finished his breakfast. He seemed paler than he had the previous night, but Gautier supposed that may have been because he had not had time to use the cosmetics in his bathroom. On the other hand, it may have been a sign that he had slept badly. Perhaps his courage, like his colouring, was only skin-deep.

'Well, Inspector, have you discovered from where that snake came?' he asked Gautier truculently.

25

'Not as yet, Monsieur, but we will. I am confident of that. And enquiries are even now being made to find out how it was brought into the hotel and smuggled into your bed.'

'So? And in the meantime, what am I supposed to do?' De Périgord's sarcasm may have been a façade to hide his fear. 'Expose myself to another attack on my life?'

'We will do all we can to protect you. Police officers are already on duty outside the hotel. If you so wish, one can be stationed in the corridor outside your suite.'

'I cannot possibly remain a prisoner in the hotel all day.'

'Then if you let me know your movements, we will do our best to make sure that you are not attacked. What are your plans for the day?'

'I shall be lunching with the Comtesse Greffulhe, and Madame Arman de Caillavet has invited me to a soirée in her home this evening.'

'And how will you travel to these appointments? By fiacre?'

'Certainly not! I have my own carriage.'

'And where will you be during the afternoon?'

'I have not yet decided.' The question appeared to irritate de Périgord. 'Look, Inspector, I cannot possibly account to you for my movements in advance! My life is not planned like a railway timetable.'

Gautier decided he would try another line of approach. 'It would help us if you could suggest who might be trying to kill you.'

'The quality of a man is revealed not by the number of his friends but by the number of his enemies. So you will not be surprised to know that I have many.'

'Not all of them, surely, would go so far as to kill you?'

De Périgord hesitated. The man was a poseur, Gautier could see that, but behind the posing, he could sense a genuine fear. In spite of that, he was reluctant to take the police into his confidence. Finally he said, 'You must understand, Inspector, that this is a political matter.'

'Political?'

'I have rendered our Government certain services of a very delicate nature. A certain foreign power may well

26

feel that the time has come to put an end to my activities, that I know too much.'

'Can you say which foreign power?'

De Périgord shrugged. 'If I were to tell you that, my life would be in even greater jeopardy.'

They talked for a few more minutes, but Gautier realized that there was nothing to be gained from prolonging their conversation. He had learned little of any value and suspected that what de Périgord had told him was less than the truth. So he left, but on his way out of the hotel stopped to have a word with Rodier, the concierge. Rodier was the doyen of the concierges in the great hotels of Paris. A man of dignity and presence, he wore his dark-red frock coat not as a badge of servitude but as a general might show off his uniform. His discretion and his ability to arrange almost anything a guest might conceivably want, had made him the friend and confidant of dukes and millionaires, bishops and actresses.

'Your men are talking to our staff one by one,' he told Gautier. 'A room has been put at their disposal for the purpose.'

'And you? You have no idea of how the snake came to be in Monsieur de Périgord's suite?'

'None.' Rodier paused and looked at Gautier as though he was uncertain of whether he should say what was on his mind. Then he continued, 'There was just one thing which perhaps I should mention. Not long ago, a man came to the hotel and made enquiries about Monsieur de Périgord.'

'A Frenchman?'

'He gave his name as Monsieur Montbrun, which is certainly a French name, and he spoke excellent French, but yet one could detect something foreign, American perhaps, in his manners. His dress, too, had an American flavour; his cravat was a little more ostentatious than most Frenchmen would prefer, and he wore a soft hat with a turned-up brim. At the time, I wondered whether he might be a Frenchman who had lived in the United States. I thought nothing of it until I saw him again soon afterwards, walking through the hotel foyer. His behaviour was suspicious.'

'Did you mention this to Monsieur de Périgord?'

'I did, and he seemed alarmed. He told me that under no circumstances would he agree to see the man. If the man ever asked for him, I should let him know, so he could leave the hotel by the back entrance.'

'If he visits the hotel again let me know. In the meantime, you can be sure that our officers will be discreet.'

'They have been and so have our staff.' Rodier lowered his voice as he added, 'As far as I can tell, none of the other guests in the hotel know of last night's unfortunate business.'

'The Englishman and his wife were not disturbed by the noise of the other maid's screams, then?'

'No, Monsieur. At least they made no mention of it when they left this morning.'

'They have left the hotel?'

'Yes. I understand that Monsieur Locke was required to return to London on a business matter of some urgency.'

Chapter 4

'Did I see you reading a newspaper as we were arriving?' Froissart asked Gautier.

'I was filling in time until you came.'

'We could forgive you if you had chosen a reputable paper,' Duthrey said.

'You mean *Figaro*?'

'Preferably.'

The Café Corneille was in Boulevard St Germain, and when Gautier had arrived ten minutes or so earlier, none of the small circle of friends who met at the café at around noon on most days were there. So, in the hope that it might help to improve his English, he had begun reading a copy of the Paris edition of the *New York Herald*.

Duthrey picked up the paper, which was lying on the table around which they were sitting. 'Now I understand. This is all part of your passion for the English,' he teased Gautier, and then turning to Froissart, he added, 'Gautier pretends that he is learning the language to further his career.'

'His career?' Froissart joined in the gentle mockery. 'Or his ambitions with that beautiful English girl whom he escorts so gallantly?'

'The lady is Irish, and I regret to say she is leaving Paris to return to Ireland this afternoon.'

Gautier was not sorry when the arrival of two more of their circle, an elderly judge and a young lawyer who was beginning to make a name for himself in politics, put an end to the banter, though not to the conversation. Most of the cafés in Paris drew their customers mainly from a

29

particular profession. There were cafés for bankers and professors and actors and jewellers and almost any other *métier* one might mention. The Café Corneille was unusual as it drew its *habitués* from a wider circle. Duthrey was a journalist on *Figaro*, Froissart had a shop selling rare books and also published in a small way, mainly the work of young, aspiring poets from the Left Bank. They might well be joined later that morning by the deputy from Val-de-Marne and the manager of the Châtelet Theatre.

'What offering has the Paris *Herald* for us today?' the young lawyer asked. 'Fashion or farce? Or hints on correct table manners?'

'Perhaps another day in the life of Nana, the poodle,' Froissart suggested.

He was referring to a story which the Paris *Herald* had once published about a dog which had its own room, bath and tutor, as well as a private maid who cooked special meals for it to be served on silver platters. The paper, which had been first published some twenty years previously, mainly for Americans living in or visiting Paris, had a reputation for lightweight stories. The French in general mocked it, although conceding that it was the most serious of the frivolous newspapers.

'Once again today,' Gautier told the others, 'we have another instalment on the Castellane saga.'

'What has Comte Boni done this time? Built another mansion or bought another yacht?'

'Those days are ended since his wife left him,' Gautier replied. 'Now the *Paris Herald* gives us the sordid details of what his extravagance cost her. Fifteen million francs already spent, and another twenty-two million in unsettled debts.'

'She was crazy to have married him,' Duthrey remarked.

'People say that she plans to marry the Prince de Sagan as soon as she has divorced Boni,' said the lawyer. He was always *au fait* with gossip and rumours of marital infidelities in Paris society, and no doubt they brought him profitable business.

30

'Will that mean another duel? Comte Boni will fight anyone to protect his dishonour,' the judge commented acidly.

'And on the most trivial excuses,' Duthrey said. 'As you know he even fought our editor.'

'I mean no disrespect to the editor of *Figaro*, but Boni chooses his opponents carefully. He preferred not to cross swords with Armand de Périgord when he accused him of usurping his family name.'

'When was that?' Gautier asked.

The lawyer explained that Comte Boni de Castellane was closely related through his mother to the Talleyrand de Périgord family, one of the oldest of the aristocratic dynasties in France. When Armand de Périgord first appeared in Paris, everyone had assumed that he too came from a branch of the same family. Then Comte Boni discovered he was a nobody, just a man named Périgord who had slipped a 'de' in front of his name as many others had done.

'Boni accused him of being an impostor, of fraud even, but he never made the accusations to his face,' the lawyer concluded.

'Why not?'

'My dear fellow, de Périgord is recognized to be one of the finest swordsmen in France.'

'He hardly looks like one.'

'Don't be deceived by his effeminacy. They say he practises at least once a week in the Club des Mousquetaires and can hold his own with the Maître des Armes there. He is an expert pistol shot as well.'

Gautier wondered whether the Comte de Castellane might be one of the many enemies whom Armand de Périgord boasted of having. Only seldom did he ever learn anything at the Café Corneille which might help him in a criminal investigation, and he never went there with that purpose. Police officers were not generally welcome in Paris cafés, largely because the Government had been known to use them to spy on suspected anarchists and other malcontents, or even as *agents provocateurs*. Gautier took it as a compliment that he had been received

31

into the small circle of friends at the Café Corneille, and he had a self-imposed rule never to discuss police matters there. Even so, what he had learned by chance that morning about de Périgord might be useful.

'The Paris *Herald* claims,' he told the others, 'that Sarah Bernhardt is planning another tour of the United States.'

'I don't believe it! She made a farewell tour there not much more than a year ago.'

They began talking about Bernhardt, who most Frenchmen believed to be the greatest actress in the world, perhaps the greatest ever. Although now well into her sixties and partly crippled, she had recently been audacious enough to play Prince Charming in *La Belle au bois dormant*. Now the Paris *Herald* hinted that before she left for America she intended to play Jeanne d'Arc, a girl of nineteen. Bernhardt's only rival on the stage was the Italian actress, Eleonora Duse, who not long previously had herself announced that she was retiring from acting. Froissart, who had seen both actresses on the stage, preferred the style of Duse.

'Bernhardt relies on a repertoire of well-practised devices and tricks, which are effective but superficial,' he said. 'Duse's performances, on the other hand, are impersonations in the true sense of the word. She acts a role naturally, lives it, becomes the character for as long as the play lasts.'

The judge agreed. 'Yes. When a play is over, Duse is emotionally exhausted. Sarah just throws kisses at the audience and prances off into the arms of her latest lover.'

After a time, the subject of their conversation switched to politics. Opinion in France was still divided over the wisdom of signing the Entente Cordiale. The French were curiously ambivalent in their attitude to the English. They imitated their style of dress and life, formed gentlemen's clubs, went racing, hunted foxes, and even had their suits made and their shirts laundered in London, but could not shake off their suspicions of 'perfidious Albion'. Some young people, not old enough to remember the humiliation of defeat by Germany in 1870, believed that a Franco-German alliance might be the best basis for peace in Europe.

When the group in the café began to break up and leave, Gautier walked with Duthrey along Boulevard St Germain to where they might find a fiacre. Duthrey was mildly irritated because that day he would not be able to linger over the excellent lunch which his wife would have waiting for him and which he liked to follow with a short nap.

'My colleague on *Figaro* who writes the financial features is indisposed,' he grumbled. 'So I am being sent in his place to interview an English banker this afternoon.'

'Which banker is that?'

'His name is Sigmund Locke. He was recently made a *Grand Officier* of the Légion d'honneur for his services to France, an unusual honour for an Englishman.'

'I had heard that Monsieur Locke had returned to England.'

'That cannot be. Originally I was told to meet him at the Hôtel Meurice, but only this morning we had a message rearranging the venue of the appointment to the Ritz.'

Back at Sûreté headquarters, Gautier found Surat waiting for him. He could tell at once from the man's manner that his visit to the Sorbonne had been fruitful and that he had news which he was waiting impatiently to tell. Surat could never disguise his excitement nor restrain his enthusiasm.

'The snake was an Egyptian cobra,' he told Gautier, 'not one of the Indian variety as the doctor believed. "*Naja naja*" they call it now, but it is also thought to be the same species as the asp, the snake that Cleopatra clasped to her bosom. Another interesting fact is that snakes are deaf to sounds carried by air. It is not the music of the snake charmer they respond to, but his movements.'

'What else did Professor Léon have to say?'

'The venom which the snake injects kills the victim by depressing or stopping the action of the heart or lungs. Even so, snake bites are not always fatal. A victim's chances of survival are high and more often than not it is fear that kills the person who has been bitten; either that or the drastic treatments which are commonly used.'

Gautier found himself thinking that a little science could be a dangerous thing. In this instance, Surat was so fascinated by what he had learnt about snakes, that he had lost sight of the purpose of the enquiries he was making. Poor Yvette, the hotel maid, was dead, and information on the chances of her surviving a snake bite was valueless. Gently, he steered Surat's enthusiasm into more productive channels.

'Has Professor Léon any idea of where the snake may have come from?'

'He has, *patron*. A Monsieur Colbert returned from East Africa only a day or two ago bringing cobras with him.'

'Marcel Colbert, the explorer?'

'Yes, *patron*. He had been asked to bring the snakes back with him for the Institut Pasteur, where they are trying to develop an antidote for snake bites.'

'Excellent! Then this afternoon, go to the Institut and find out whether one of their snakes is missing, and if so, who might have taken it.'

The list of guests staying at the Hôtel Meurice the previous night, which the management had prepared for Gautier, had arrived and lay on his desk. He and Surat studied it together. A large proportion of the guests were English, as a party had arrived from London for the race meeting at Longchamps, which was being held that afternoon and would continue for the next three days. The aristocracy was well represented in the party, with one duke, one viscount, three baronets and a number of men and women whose names were prefixed with the words 'The Honourable'.

'What does this word "honourable" signify?' Surat asked Gautier. 'Is it a decoration like the Légion d'honneur?'

'Not exactly. In most cases, it is a hereditary title.'

'Do the British not have a Légion d'honneur?'

34

'No. One must assume that they do not have as much honour as we French and so cannot dispense it as liberally as we do.'

Making jokes about the British love of titles was, Gautier reflected, a little unfair, for no nation had a greater passion for decorations than the French. The various grades of the Légion d'honneur were handed out so lavishly that there were now more than 40,000 *chevaliers*, 6,000 *officiers* and 1,000 *commandeurs*. On top of this, France had a whole string of orders of merit and commemorative medals for people in different professions and *métiers*: for farmers, schoolteachers, municipal police, customs officials, post-office clerks and even porters in Les Halles.

Half-way down the hotel's list was a name which seemed familiar. The copy of the Paris *Herald* which Gautier had taken to the Café Corneille lay on his desk, and flicking through it, he saw why. Kurt Goesler was a German musician of international reputation who, the *Herald* reported, was in Paris to give a series of concerts. The music critic of the *Herald* assured his readers that Goesler was one of the greatest performers on the French horn, unrivalled in Europe and possibly in the world. The name and the musical instrument sparked off an idea in Gautier's mind.

'This man Goesler plays the French horn,' he told Surat. 'A strange instrument, basically only one long tube which, if uncoiled, would not be unlike the shape of a snake.'

'What are you thinking?'

'That the case in which a French horn is carried, if empty, would be ideal for carrying a concealed snake.'

'You're not suggesting that this musician put the snake in de Périgord's bed?'

'Not at all. The idea I have is improbable, far-fetched, one might say, but it might be worth further examination.'

Since his short visit to Paris was supposed to be incognito, Monsieur Windsor was not travelling on a royal train, but would be returning to London that afternoon on the boat train belonging to the Compagnie des Wagons Lits. The precautions that had been taken to ensure his safety were unspectacular, no more than might be arranged for any traveller of importance or wealth. One whole carriage of the train had been reserved for him and his companions, and Gautier learned that three officers from London's Metropolitan Police in plain clothes would be aboard.

The platform of the Gare du Nord from which the train would be leaving was crowded with Parisians who had come to see off their friends. Monsieur Windsor had not yet arrived, but Gautier knew that when he did, the Director General of the Sûreté would be in attendance, as well, no doubt, as a number of discreetly anonymous senior French Government officials. Gautier had already spoken to Claire Ryan, and she was now talking excitedly to the French ladies of her own age, who had known her at the finishing school in Switzerland which she had attended several years previously and who had come to see her leave. Only the Earl of Newry stood alone on the platform and Gautier went to join him.

After they had chatted for a while, the Earl said, 'Claire owes you a great debt of gratitude, Monsieur Gautier, and so do I.'

'What makes you say that, Monsieur?'

'You have done so much for Claire these last few weeks.' Gautier wondered how much the Earl knew of his relationship with Claire and whether there might be a hidden innuendo in the remark, but the Earl continued, 'You have shown her so much of Paris that a single girl on her own would never have seen. She loves France and the French.'

'I sense that, but even so, she is glad to be going home.'

'Excited, yes, but the excitement will pass and then she will miss Paris. Still, I have to send her home.'

They strolled along the platform towards where Claire stood with her friends. Gautier guessed that the Earl had more to say and was wondering how best to express it. Eventually, he asked a question, 'Are you aware that Claire is not just my housekeeper?'

'Yes, Monsieur. She explained to me the circumstances of her birth.'

When they had made love for the first time, Claire had explained to Gautier that her mother had lived in a village on the Earl's estate in Ireland. She had also told him that the Countess of Newry, a rich American, had refused to allow the Earl to bring Claire up as his daughter. That was why she had been sent first to boarding school and then to a finishing school in Switzerland, before finding work as a children's governess. When the Countess had divorced the Earl and he had come to live in Paris, Claire had been passed off as his housekeeper. It was too late for him suddenly to produce a grown-up daughter.

'Through my fault, the girl has had so little from life,' the Earl said. 'I must at least find her a husband.'

'In Ireland?'

'Yes. To marry a Frenchman she would need a dowry, which I am not in a position to provide. In Ireland, bachelors outnumber unmarried girls and there are plenty of good, dependable men – farmers, solicitors, accountants – who expect only that a girl should be a good wife and mother.'

They had almost reached Claire and her friends, and when she saw them she came over towards them. 'We must go and find our compartment,' she told her father. 'The train will be leaving at any minute.' Then she faced Gautier. 'How can I ever thank you, Jean-Paul?'

'It is I who have to thank you.'

'I shall miss you.'

She held out her hand for him to kiss, but then changed her mind impulsively, threw her arms around him and kissed him on the cheek as she hugged him. Her Parisian friends, who were watching, smiled at this display of what they probably saw as Celtic warmth. Only Gautier would have seen the tears in her eyes.

She pulled her father away and they boarded the train, leaving Gautier alone. Looking back along the platform, he saw that Monsieur Windsor and his party had arrived and were boarding their private carriage, which was towards the end of the train. Courtrand was with them, fussing attentively and giving orders to the porters who were handling their valises. The Prefect of Police, to whom Courtrand and all other police functionaries in Paris were responsible, had also come to the Gare du Nord for the occasion.

As he waited for the boat train to pull out of the station, Gautier thought about the reason why Claire was being taken home. Had the Earl of Newry been suggesting that he would like to have found a Frenchman who would marry her without a dowry? Had he been hinting that Gautier might be willing to marry her? At first sight, the idea seemed highly unlikely, absurd even, but Gautier did not dismiss it out of hand. When he had married, his wife Suzanne had brought him a generous dowry, for her father had a good wholesale crockery business, but now he was no longer a young man starting married life and a career. Should he, a widower moving towards middle age, expect a dowry?

For a brief moment he tried to imagine himself married to Claire. Then he put the fantasy aside, reminding himself that his marriage to Suzanne had failed. One had to accept, he supposed, that some men should never marry.

Although all the passengers were aboard, for some reason the departure of the train was being delayed. On the platform outside the royal party's special carriage, the stationmaster in his top-hat and frock coat was waving instructions to the guard. As he waited, Gautier saw the Prefect of Police approaching him. The Prefect was an amiable man whom Gautier had always admired. In a small way, he was an eccentric, inclined to treat the strict conventions of society with a light-hearted disdain. His style of dress bordered on the informal, he did not sport a beard or moustaches, and he was reputed to have had at one time a pretty African girl as his mistress. Behind his façade of insouciance, though, there was a shrewd and perceptive brain. He thought highly of Gautier, consulted him unofficially from time to time, and had more than once intervened when Courtrand, through pettiness or jealousy, had threatened to discipline him.

As he reached Gautier, the boat train began to pull away from the platform. 'Like me, Gautier,' he remarked, 'you are probably relieved to see our royal visitor leaving us safe and in good health.'

'Yes, Monsieur le Préfet. He is such a considerate gentleman and such a friend of France, that he deserves to enjoy his little vacations with us in peace.'

'I agree. The poor fellow must need to escape occasionally from the stifling conventions of the English court.'

The two men watched the train leave, and then began walking up the platform towards the station's exit. The Prefect said, 'What will you do now about your English lessons?'

Gautier had realized that the Prefect was aware that he was taking English lessons, it may well have been his idea that he should, but not that he knew Claire Ryan had been giving them. He was not surprised, though, for the Prefect kept himself informed, unobtrusively, about the personal lives and problems of those who worked under him. The sympathetic tone of his question suggested that he also knew that Gautier was losing not only a teacher but what a Frenchman might call his '*petite amie*'.

'I shall look for another teacher, Monsieur.'

'Yes, do, Gautier. More than ever now, with the invasion of France from across the Atlantic as well as the Channel, it is important that we should have at least one senior officer in the Sûreté with a good command of English.'

As they walked, they talked of the growing number of Anglo-Saxons who were arriving in continental Europe. In the previous year, the Prefect told Gautier, more than three hundred thousand Americans alone were known to be in Europe, and the vast majority of them would at least pass through Paris. Wealthy Americans – the Vanderbilts, Whitneys, Astors and Pierpont Morgans – were arriving in France to rent magnificent homes in Paris, buy pictures, restore châteaux in the provinces, race their horses at Longchamps. Paris had become the social as well as the cultural capital of the world.

'As it happens,' the Prefect remarked to Gautier, 'I may be able to help you in the matter of an English teacher. Do you know Madame Catriona Becker?'

'I have never met the lady, but I have heard of her.'

'Because of that business over the death of her husband?'

'Yes, although I was not personally involved in the investigation.'

Madame Becker was the widow of a Belgian living in Paris, and her husband's death two or three years previously had caused a minor gust of scandal in the rarefied atmosphere of Paris society. The circumstances of Monsieur Becker's death had been sufficiently suspicious to warrant an investigation by the Sûreté, but no evidence of any criminal act had been found. The newspapers and the gossips had lost interest and the scandal had blown itself out.

'I believe Madame Becker would welcome an opportunity to give you tuition in English,' the Prefect said. 'She is Scottish by birth, you know.'

'But why should she wish to? Did her husband not leave her a sizeable fortune?'

'Not as sizeable as people believed and she has been careless with her money. Madame Becker has been a good friend of mine for a long time and I would like to help her.'

The Prefect's remark sounded casual enough, but Gautier had the feeling that he was asking a favour. 'Do you think I should approach her to see whether she would be interested in giving me lessons?'

'I would be obliged if you were to do so. Would you like me to make an appointment for you to see her?'

Gautier knew now that the Prefect was not asking a favour but giving instructions. Intuition told him that this was not just a matter of providing a society lady with a little pocket money, and no doubt in due course he would learn what motive lay behind the Prefect's intervention.

They parted outside the Gare du Nord, the Prefect leaving for his office in a carriage that had been waiting for him, and Gautier boarding an omnibus. He had an affection for horse-drawn omnibuses, as a symbol of a leisurely life that was disappearing and one which he might not be able to enjoy much longer, for there was a move to replace them with motor buses. The omnibus took him to Boulevard Haussmann, from where he walked past the Opéra and made his way to Place Vendôme. The journey would have been speedier in a fiacre, but he was in no hurry, for he believed it unlikely that Duthrey would as yet have finished interviewing Sigmund Locke.

To waste a little more time he made a tour around Place Vendôme, circling the column which had been built to commemorate Napoleon's victory at Austerlitz and topped with a statue of the Emperor himself. During the abortive revolt of the Commune after France's disastrous defeat by Germany in 1871, a mob, led by the painter Gustave Courbet, had pulled down the column. In due course, it and the statue had been reconstructed, and Courbet had been convicted for his part in the affair and sentenced to so large a fine to pay for the work that he had been forced to spend the rest of his life in exile. Glancing up at it, Gautier reflected that the French had a passion for grandiose gestures, whose symbolism never matched their futility.

When eventually he arrived at the Ritz, Duthrey must have left, for the concierge sent a page up to Sigmund Locke's suite with Gautier's visiting card. A few minutes later, he was told that Monsieur Locke would see him, and he was taken up to the banker's suite on the second floor of the hotel.

Locke was a dark man who was carrying too much flesh for his frame, and had a large head with huge jowls. The pince-nez he was wearing only seemed to intensify the austere aloofness in his eyes.

'As you can see, Inspector, I have just had some tea brought up,' he told Gautier. 'May I offer you a cup?'

Gautier accepted. If he was to understand the English,

41

he must appreciate their tastes and their habits. Locke poured him a cup of tea from the silver tea service, and added milk and sugar.

'How can I help you, Inspector?'

'Thank you for sparing the time to see me, Monsieur. I am enquiring into an incident which took place at the Hôtel Meurice last night. Are you acquainted with Monsieur Armand de Périgord?'

'I know of him, of course, and I know he lives at the Meurice, but we have never been formally introduced.'

As far as Gautier could tell, there was no hint of disapproval in Locke's reply, but bankers, he supposed, became skilled at concealing their feelings. Gautier told him of the snake that had been found in de Périgord's bedroom and of the death of the chambermaid.

'I wondered, Monsieur, whether you might have heard anything during the night,' he concluded. 'The maid's screams, for instance. Or whether you may have seen anyone in the corridor earlier in the evening. Your suite was on the same floor as that of Monsieur de Périgord, I understand.'

'I regret I cannot help you. I neither heard nor saw anything,' Locke replied. Then he added, 'I should explain to you, Monsieur Gautier, that I sleep badly, suffering as I do from rheumatism. So I always take a sleeping draught when I retire.'

'And your wife?'

'If she had heard anything, I am sure she would have told me.'

'Even so, would it be possible for us to ask her?'

'Unhappily no. Madame Locke returned to England this afternoon. She took the boat train from the Gare du Nord.'

Chapter 5

As he walked from the Ritz to Sûreté headquarters in Quai des Orfèvres, Gautier was thinking about Madame Locke. He had no reason to believe that Locke had not been telling the truth about his wife's return to London, but if she had been on the boat train, Locke could not have been at the station to see her leave, as he was being interviewed by Duthrey. Was it being too fanciful to suspect that she had been smuggled out of France, quietly and hastily? Gautier remembered the story which the night porter had told him of Madame Locke's visit to de Périgord's suite late at night. There were questions to be asked about that, but Madame Locke was out of reach, at least for the present, so he filed them away in a compartment of his mind as one might a letter to be answered later.

When he reached his office, he found two reports on his desk, one from Surat and the other from the officer whom he had put in charge of the enquiries at the Hôtel Meurice. He was amused by the pretentious title that Surat had given his report, but as he began reading it, he realized that his enquiries had been efficient and fruitful.

CONFIDENTIAL REPORT   For Chief Inspector Gautier

The Affair of the Missing Cobra

Officials at the Institut Pasteur report that they received three live cobras from Monsieur Marcel Colbert. They had been expecting four, but since Monsieur Colbert was bringing the snakes back from

Africa as a favour and was asking for no payment beyond the cost of transporting the beasts, have not thought to complain nor even comment on the discrepancy. At my request, they checked and were able to confirm that all three snakes are alive and well in their laboratories.

Monsieur Colbert was not in when I called at his home in Passy, as he was giving a lecture to a geographical society. However, I was able to question his assistant, a Monsieur Emil Bey, who makes all the arrangements for Colbert's journeys of exploration. Bey explained that Colbert had sent four snakes back from Africa during his last trip there, but that one had died in transit. When I began to question Bey about the snake's demise, he grew at first evasive and then truculent. I formed the strong impression that the man, who seems to be of Egyptian origin although educated in France, was not being truthful and that he has something to conceal.

Surat

The report of the officer in charge of the enquiries at the Hôtel Meurice was more factual and precise. Staff at the hotel had confirmed that early the previous evening, a representative of a company of musical instrument suppliers had arrived at the hotel, carrying a French horn which, he said, was one of Herr Goesler's spare instruments and which the company had been repairing. The man had refused to leave the instrument with the concierge, saying that it was extremely valuable and could easily be damaged. So a page had taken him up to Goesler's suite, opened the door with a passkey and allowed him to leave the instrument inside the room. After hearing this, the police officer had spoken to Goesler, who had denied having sent a French horn for repair or that he had found one in his suite when he returned to the hotel that night. Enquiries were continuing to establish the name of the musical instrument company and the identity of the man who had visited the Hôtel Meurice.

After reading the reports, Gautier jotted down some instructions on each of them. He told Surat that he should bring the explorer's assistant to Sûreté headquarters the following morning for questioning. What he wanted done at the Hôtel Meurice was less straightforward. He was convinced now that the snake must have been smuggled into the hotel hidden in the French horn's carrying case. Tracing the man who had taken it there might not be easy and would take time. But the case had been left in Monsieur Goesler's suite, and someone must have moved it and the snake from there to the suite of Armand de Périgord. That could only have been done by someone who had, or had borrowed or stolen, a passkey which would give access to both suites. To trace that individual, the police officers carrying out the investigation would have once again to question all the hotel staff, and particularly chambermaids, waiters and any other staff employed in cleaning or providing room service. Almost as an afterthought, he added that the concierge should be asked whether he had seen or heard anything of Monsieur Montbrun again.

Gautier had just finished writing these instructions, when the electric bell in his office rang. He was surprised to hear it, for Courtrand seldom worked later than the middle of the afternoon, and Gautier had assumed that he would not have returned to Sûreté headquarters from the Gare du Nord after seeing the boat train leave. However, not only was the Director General in his office but in an excellent humour.

'Our royal visitor very much enjoyed his little holiday in Paris,' he told Gautier, 'and made a point of thanking me for the discretion and courtesy which was extended to him while he was here.'

'That is good to know, Monsieur.'

'I think we may congratulate ourselves on having helped to cement even further the friendship between our country and England.' Gautier restrained a smile. Before long Courtrand would have convinced himself that he personally had engineered the Entente Cordiale. Courtrand went on, 'Some of the credit must go to you, Gautier, but we must not allow ourselves to become complacent. Monsieur Windsor will return to Paris before long. We may be sure of that.'

'You believe so?'

'Why not? Even at his age he remains a virile man and it would appear that only in Paris can he find what he needs. We must be prepared for his next visit.'

'Have you anything particular in mind which we should be doing?'

'The Comte de Chartres must not be allowed to make any more demonstrations, however ineffective. What do you know about the man?'

'Very little.'

'I have been making some enquiries about him myself. The man is a fool. He has become obsessed with jealousy over the flirtation which his wife had with the Prince of Wales years ago, but is unaware that she is being unfaithful to him now.'

'With whom?'

'No one knows, but the rumour is so persistent that it must be true. Everyone in Paris is laughing at him.'

'Would it help if we knew?'

'Possibly. One might then be able to deflect his jealousy from Monsieur Windsor.'

'If you wish, I could make discreet enquiries.'

'No, Gautier. I shall handle this affair myself. I shall have a file opened on the Comte de Chartres and have him kept under a general surveillance.'

Gautier was glad he was not being asked to find out the name of the man who was making a *cocu* of the Comte de Chartres. Secret passions, intrigue and adultery were part of life in Paris, and so was the gossip they inspired. Sometimes it became necessary for the Sûreté to listen to the gossip and keep a watch on the liaisons, but it was an aspect of police work which he did not enjoy.

When, after leaving Courtrand, he returned to his own office, he found a pale envelope waiting for him, a letter

46

that had been delivered by hand only a few minutes earlier. The note it contained was handwritten in a flowery but immature script.

Monsieur,
My friend the Prefect of Police tells me that you would like to speak with me on a private matter. I shall be at home this evening between six-thirty and seven and would be happy to receive you then, if it were convenient. Please accept my most distinguished sentiments.

Catriona Becker

Gautier pulled out his pocket watch and saw that he would have to leave the Sûreté almost immediately if he were to keep the appointment. He was intrigued by the speed with which the Prefect of Police had acted, for his need to renew his English studies was in no way pressing.

On his way downstairs he remembered Madame Locke. Her hasty and, for him, inconvenient departure from Paris was another thing which intrigued him. As part of the security precautions taken to protect Monsieur Windsor, the Sûreté had obtained from the Gare du Nord a list of all the passengers who had reserved berths on the boat train. He took a look at the list in the office downstairs before he left the Sûreté. The name of a Madame Locke had been written in ink at the bottom of the typewritten list, obviously as a late addition. Against the name was a note, 'Travelling as Madame Smith'.

Madame Catriona Becker had an apartment in a street leading off Boulevard Haussmann. Gautier recalled that when her husband died, they had been living in Faubourg St Germain, a district on the Left Bank facing the Louvre and the Jardin des Tuileries, where the élite of Paris society preferred to reside. As he climbed the stairs to the apartment, which was on the second floor of the building, he wondered whether her move might have been

47

dictated by a need to economize. The Prefect of Police had suggested that she had been careless with the money her husband had left her. On the other hand, for a widow without children to live on her own in an *hôtel particulier* would have been wildly extravagant. Madame Becker was Scottish, and Gautier had always heard the Scots were a thrifty race.

The elderly maid who opened the door to him was clearly not French, and her accent suggested that she too might be Scottish. She told Gautier that her mistress was expecting him and led him into the salon of the apartment, where he found Madame Becker reclining on a *chaise-longue*. His first thought was how like Claire Ryan she looked and he was mildly irritated. Claire had left and he had no wish to be reminded of her so soon. Then, as he approached Madame Becker, he saw that the resemblance between the two women was only superficial, a similarity in colouring and complexion, but not in other features or build. Catriona Becker was shorter and more sturdy than Claire and gave an immediate impression of restless energy.

'How kind of you to come.' She held out her hand for Gautier to kiss. 'And at such short notice.'

'I am obliged to you, Madame, for agreeing to see me, and to the Prefect of Police for arranging it.'

'Ah, the Prefect,' Madame Becker said dreamily, and allowed the words to hang in the air.

When Gautier realized that she had nothing to add to them, he said, 'He suggested that you might be willing to give me lessons in English.'

'Ah yes, English. Tell me about your English, Inspector. Who has been teaching you?'

'An Irish lady from the household of the Earl of Newry. She has been living in Paris, but returned to Ireland today.'

'A Celt, like myself. What did she teach you?'

'Not very much, I regret to say. The lessons she gave me were few in number and obviously I am a slow learner.'

'It sounds as though she may not have been using the most rapid method of instruction,' Madame Becker said,

48

smiling. 'But let us find out how much you know. I shall speak a few simple phrases in French for you to repeat in English, if you are able to.'

She began calling out simple sentences: greetings, expressions of gratitude, the ordinary day-to-day questions one might ask through courtesy. Gautier found he could manage them in English, although he knew his accent was laughable.

'You've made a good start anyway. But I suppose you are learning the language to assist you in your professional duties. Now I will test your knowledge of the kind of words you will need to know; your vocabulary of crime, one might say.'

Now Madame Becker began calling out French words, one at a time, for him to translate into English; words like 'arrest', 'indictment', 'prison', 'judge', 'theft', 'assault'. Eventually, she came to one for which Gautier did not know the equivalent, the French word *'chantage'*.

'We say "blackmail" in English,' she told him.

'An interesting derivation!'

'No more so than for the French word.' She seemed to hesitate before going on to ask him, 'Do you come across it often in your work?'

'No, not often.'

'Could that be because the French are not susceptible to blackmail? Perhaps they do not value their reputations so highly as, for example, the Americans.'

'Perhaps. Or it could be that the indiscretions for which people are usually blackmailed do not seem so reprehensible to us French; adultery, for example, or a little modest fraud.'

'That is a very cynical remark!' Madame Becker laughed. 'But I am being very inhospitable, Monsieur Gautier. May I offer you a glass of something? A whisky, perhaps?'

'You are very kind. I accept with pleasure.'

A bell stood on the small table beside her *chaise-longue*, and as Madame Becker picked it up and rang it, she asked Gautier, 'You've tasted whisky before, then?'

49

'Only on rare occasions, but I have heard that it helps one with learning languages by lubricating the tongue.'

'Did your Irish friend never offer you whisky?'

'Never. So far as I know, she never drank whisky, nor did the Earl of Newry.'

'That would be because they are gentry. The gentry in Ireland prefer to drink brandy.' Madame Becker seemed to hesitate, and then she added quickly, 'Or so I've heard. In Scotland, though, whisky is the universal drink; even for women.'

As she was speaking, the maid who had let Gautier into the apartment came into the room. She must have known what her mistress would be wanting, for she was carrying a decanter of whisky and two glasses on a silver tray. After placing the tray on the table beside the *chaise-longue*, she left the room.

'You will have realized that I come of farming stock,' Madame Becker said as she was pouring the whisky.

'I find that hard to believe.'

'It's true. My father owns a tiny farm in the Highlands of Scotland.'

She began talking about her parents, her childhood and life on a farm just outside the tiny village of Tomintoul. Possibly she may have sensed that Gautier was wondering how, with her humble origins, she had managed to become a fashionable hostess in Paris – elegant, expensively coutured, sophisticated. Education in Scotland was the finest in Europe, she told him, and she had been well equipped with knowledge and good manners when she went to work, first in London and then in Belgium.

'And in Belgium you met Monsieur Becker?'

'Yes, I was fortunate. He was a good man; much older than me, which is why we never had children.'

'You must miss him now, Madame.'

'I do. You have no idea how difficult life is for a widow in Paris. If I were ten years older, things would be different.' Madame Becker gave a short, bitter laugh. 'But why am I telling you what you must already know? The police scrutinized every aspect of my life, every detail, when I

50

was suspected of having murdered Bertrand.'

'I was not involved in that investigation.'

Gautier's reply seemed to please Madame Becker, lifting her discontent. She said cheerfully, 'Anyway, soon I shall be a widow no longer.'

'You plan to remarry?'

'Yes. An American from Pittsburgh.'

'When will that be?'

'In a few weeks. Wayne intends to settle in France, and he has returned home to make the necessary financial arrangements.'

As they drank their whisky, she told Gautier about the man who she was to marry. Wayne Archer was one son of a Methodist family which had made a fortune out of a huge pig farm and then invested their money in a Pittsburgh steelworks. Although not yet forty, he did not need to work for a living, and wished to spend his wealth on building a collection of paintings and sculptures and on charitable bequests. Much of his money was tied up in a trust, and he had returned to America to negotiate with the trustees and secure an income sufficient for a life in Paris.

'Like many Americans, Wayne has strong religious prejudices. His family are strict Methodists. He would never marry a Catholic, but I, of course, belong to the Presbyterian Church.'

Madame Becker did not match Gautier's idea of a Presbyterian. He had always heard that the Church of Scotland was strict and humourless, denying its members any of the pleasures which Catholics were allowed – good wine, dancing and, after celebrating Mass, carefree, joyful Sabbaths. Madame Becker had the air of someone who would enjoy all these. She was drinking whisky, and Gautier could tell from the lingering smell of smoke which hung in the air of the room, that she probably also smoked cigarettes, and that, as every Frenchman knew, was the mark of a daringly liberal woman.

When an opportune moment came, he steered their conversation back to the subject of his visit. 'About these

51

English lessons, Madame. Do you really believe that you might be able to spare the time to teach me?'

'Of course. We might have the first lesson tomorrow; at about this time, if that were convenient.'

'It would be for me. But we ought to discuss the matter of payment.'

'Let us leave that for the time being. I will speak to the Prefect on the subject.' Madame Becker looked at Gautier, as though she had suddenly had an idea and was uncertain of how he would respond to it. 'Instead of paying for tomorrow's lesson, you could do me a great favour, Monsieur Gautier, if you would.'

'And what is that, Madame?'

'I have been invited to dine tomorrow at the house of a very old and dear friend. It is a long-standing invitation and an occasion to which I have been looking forward eagerly. Unfortunately, the gentleman who was to escort me now finds that he cannot do so. I wonder if you would be kind enough to take his place.'

'Would that be acceptable to your hostess?'

'I am certain it would.' Madame Becker smiled. 'You have something of a reputation, Monsieur, as a charming and gallant escort. If you were to agree, I should be envied by the other ladies present.'

Now it was Gautier's turn to smile. 'How could any man resist such flattery? I shall be enchanted.'

Soon afterwards, as he was leaving Madame Becker's apartment, Gautier was thinking that her invitation to escort her to a dinner party could not have been made on a sudden impulse, but was part of a plan in which he had been picked to play a role. He wondered whether the Prefect of Police knew of the plan and approved of it.

Chapter 6

'As I have already told you, one cobra died on the journey back from Africa.'

Emil Bey, the assistant of the explorer, Marcel Colbert, was a slim, good-looking young man. His colouring as well as his name suggested that he was of Egyptian origins, but his French was faultless and free of any accent. He had made it plain that he resented having been brought to Sûreté headquarters for questioning that morning, and Gautier sensed that his resentment was only a mask for fear. As Surat had suggested in his report, Bey had something he wished to hide.

'Are you aware, Monsieur, that a young woman was killed by a cobra in a hotel two nights ago?'

'I know nothing of that.'

'If it were proved that the cobra which killed her was one of those you brought back from Africa, you would be implicated in her murder.'

'Me! How could I be? What hotel? I was not in any hotel. I haven't been in a hotel in Paris for weeks!'

'We know that the snake was smuggled into the hotel. The staff will be able to identify the man who took it in.'

'Well, it was not me.'

'Can you prove that? Where were you in the afternoon, not yesterday but the day before?'

'At home. In Monsieur Colbert's home. I live there.'

'Can anyone confirm that, Monsieur?'

To Gautier's surprise, Bey blushed. Not even the natural tan of his skin could conceal the flush. He replied reluctantly, 'Madame Colbert was in the house.'

'Then we must pursue our enquiries with the lady.'

'You must not do that, Inspector. On no account!'

'Why not?' Gautier realized that Bey was on the defensive, trapped in cross-currents of guilt and loyalty.

'You would be placing me in great difficulty. I might well lose my position.'

'I have no other choice.'

Bey hesitated for a while. 'What if I told you the truth about the cobra? Would that satisfy you?'

'It depends on what you told me.'

'I had no part in the death of any young woman. I did give away one of the cobras which we brought back from Africa. I suppose it must have been the one found in the hotel, but I know nothing of that.'

'You gave the snake away?'

'If you must know, I sold it.'

'To whom?'

Although the truth was straightforward enough, it had to be prised out of Bey. Like many people caught out in a deception, he embellished the story which he told Gautier with irrelevant details and remarks, hoping they would justify his behaviour. He had sold one of the cobras to a man named Laborde for five hundred francs. There could be no harm in that. Three snakes would be enough for the Institut Pasteur's experiments. It was Bey himself who had brought the snakes back from Africa, not Colbert, who had travelled separately. Bey had made all the transport arrangements, dealt with the tiresome formalities. Was he not entitled to a modest recompense for his trouble? He was, in any case, grossly underpaid.

When questioned about the man who had bought the snakes, Bey had to be prodded for answers. Monsieur Laborde had called on him uninvited, claiming he was an agent for a private zoo in the South of France. He had presented a business card and had been well-dressed in morning coat and top-hat. No, Bey had not kept the card. Gautier could understand why. The man had no reason for keeping any evidence which might implicate him in a transaction which he hoped would not be detected. But he had taken the five hundred francs in cash which he had been offered.

'How soon after you arrived back from Africa did this man Laborde call on you?'

'The following day.'

'Then he must have known that you would be bringing snakes back with you.'

'I suppose so.'

'How could he have known?'

Bey shrugged. 'He may have been told by someone working for the Institut Pasteur, or for the travel agent who made the transport arrangements. Monsieur Colbert may have mentioned it to one of his friends. There was no secret about our expedition to Africa.'

'And Laborde took the snake away with him?'

'Yes. He had come to the house in a fiacre and had brought a basket in which to carry it; one of those round baskets which snake charmers use.'

No amount of further questions could deflect Bey from the story he was telling, and Gautier decided that it must be the truth. The young man seemed curiously concerned to protect his employer's wife, but that need not have any relevance to the matter of the cobra. He was able to give a useful description of Monsieur Laborde: tall, slim and erect in his bearing, with light brown hair and probably in his thirties. The man's accent, Bey believed, was certainly not that of a Parisian, but had the rasp of the provinces.

When Gautier decided he had no more questions to ask, and allowed Bey to leave, he remarked to Surat, 'The description of this Monsieur Laborde is very similar to that of the man who took the French horn, or at least the case of one, to the Hôtel Meurice.'

'Do you think it is the same man?'

'Almost certainly. The whole plot could have been devised and carried out by one man. He bought the cobra from Bey and took it to the Meurice himself. What we need to know is how he was able to put it into de Périgord's bed.'

'We may find the answer to that in this report.'

On his way up to Gautier's office, Surat had collected a report which had been made out earlier that morning by the officer in charge of the enquiries at the Hôtel Meurice. Surat was right in suggesting that it might provide the answer to Gautier's question. All the hotel staff had been interviewed for a second time, and three of them, two chambermaids and a room-service waiter, recalled having seen a workman carrying a bag of plumber's tools in the vicinity of de Périgord's suite on the evening when the snake bit Yvette. From their description, it seemed certain that, although he was dressed differently, he must have been the same man who had taken the French horn case to the hotel.

'He would have needed a key to get into the two suites,' Surat commented. 'Goesler's to fetch the snake and then de Périgord's.'

'That would not have been difficult. He could have borrowed one from a chambermaid. This Monsieur Laborde is a resourceful man.'

'And an enemy of de Périgord?'

'I would not think so,' Gautier replied. 'The kind of enemies de Périgord would make, people from his social milieu, would not have sullied their hands with murder. No, it seems more likely that this Monsieur Laborde would have been hired to place the snake in de Périgord's bed.'

Gautier and Surat began to discuss what to do next. Discovering the stages in the plot which had led to the death of the chambermaid Yvette had been surprisingly simple, perhaps too simple. Tracing the man behind the plan would be far more difficult. Paris was full of criminals who could be hired to kill: apaches from Pigalle who would cut a throat for a few sous, women from the slums who had taught themselves the arts of poisoning. One should not ignore the possibility, however, that Monsieur Laborde, or whatever the man's real name might be, may have been imported to carry out the murder. Those who had spoken to him had mentioned that he had an accent which suggested the South of France. If this were true, tracking him down would be even more difficult. By this time, he might well have left Paris and returned home.

The measures which Gautier asked Surat to put in train were routine for an investigation of this type. The police *commissariats* in every *arrondissement* in Paris would be alerted and given a description of Laborde. If the man were from outside Paris, he would have needed a hotel where he could stay while he carried out his mission. Officers from the Sûreté would start calling on the mass of small hotels, concentrating in the region of the Gare du Lyon, where trains from southern France arrived and left.

'When you have made these arrangements,' Gautier told Surat, 'I suggest you go along to the Meurice yourself and question the staff who saw this man. Someone may have forgotten or overlooked some little detail which may help us. Try to speak to the staff when they are off duty if you can.'

Near the Hôtel Meurice, there would certainly be a bistro where the staff would go after finishing work, where they would drink and gossip about the hotel, the guests and their colleagues. Surat had a talent for becoming friendly with ordinary people and for winning their confidence. The porters and waiters from the Meurice would talk more freely with him after a glass of wine than they would in the hotel.

After Surat had left, Gautier picked up another report which had been lying on his desk when he arrived that morning. It had been made out by the police officers whom he had assigned to keep a watch on Armand de Périgord and give him what protection they could. Their task had been made easier, for de Périgord had been co-operative, telling the police at what time he expected to leave the Hôtel Meurice, where he was going and when he expected to return. As he had told Gautier the previous morning, he had lunched with the Comtesse Greffulhe at her home in Rue d'Astorg. In the afternoon, he had spent two hours in the Club des Mousquetaires, practising fencing, followed by an hour in a Turkish bath, returning to his hotel to change into evening dress before going to dine with Madame Arman de Caillavet. Madame de Caillavet, mistress of the author Anatole France, was a leading bourgeois hostess in Paris, and entertained poets, musicians and Government ministers, as well as members of the aristocracy at her home in Avenue Hoche.

Gautier had been surprised when de Périgord had told him that he had his own carriage to drive him in and around Paris. Fewer landaus, *calèches* or Victorias were to be seen in Paris now, and those who did not own an automobile relied on the many hundred fiacres to be found in the streets. Now Gautier learned from the report that what de Périgord had told him was not strictly true. He did not own a carriage but hired one from the Compagnie Générale des Fiacres, an arrangement which, Gautier knew, cost twelve hundred francs a month, with another one hundred and fifty francs for the coachman. Many people would feel that for a bachelor to have a carriage permanently at his disposal was an extravagant affectation, and one could only suppose that de Périgord thought it enhanced his prestige in the fashionable social circles in which he evidently moved.

Putting the report on one side, Gautier turned his attention to the day's newspapers. Copies of these were always placed on his desk each day; *Figaro* and *Le Monde* to give him the news and the Paris *Herald* to help him in his English studies. A headline above a report in *Le Monde* caught his attention.

FRENCH DIPLOMAT FOUND DEAD

His Excellency Eugène Deslandes, France's Ambassador in London, was found dead of gunshot wounds in the Kensington residence yesterday morning. A revolver was found on the floor beside the Ambassador's body.

*

Catriona Becker and Gautier were two of nine guests who dined with Princesse Hélène at her apartment in Montparnasse that evening. Like some other hostesses in Paris, the Princesse usually held a small dinner party before her soirées. After the dinner, as many as thirty people might fill her salon and overflow into the conservatory of the apartment which backed on to a small, secluded square lined with chestnut trees.

Gautier supposed that he should have been surprised to find that the explorer Marcel Colbert and his wife Léontine were among the other guests at dinner, but he had learned to suspend his surprise when faced with what appeared to be coincidences. Often they proved to be not coincidences at all but part of a complex pattern of events in which he was becoming involved.

On this occasion, the outline of the pattern was only beginning to emerge, but already there had been one development which could not be written off as coincidence. Catriona Becker and he had been driven in her carriage to the Princesse's home. On the way, she had told Gautier that the Princesse now knew he was to be her companion that evening and was delighted.

'As you can see,' Catriona remarked, 'your reputation as a gallant escort has already spread.'

'May I ask who is the unfortunate man I am replacing tonight?' he asked casually.

'Monsieur Armand de Périgord,' she replied without hesitation, but she was not looking at Gautier as she spoke. Then she added equally casually, 'Do you know him?'

Gautier wondered whether this was a cue for him to tell her about the snake that had been found in de Périgord's bed, but he decided not to. 'Only slightly.'

Princesse Hélène's invitation to Colbert and his wife that evening had been made with a purpose. Her principal guest at dinner and at the soirée to follow was Professor Henning Kastrup, a Danish scholar who had recently arrived in Paris with his wife, Greta. The professor was an anthropologist who, not long previously, had written a book putting forward a new theory on the origins and development of sexual practices among primitive tribes on the African continent. Because his theory was highly unorthodox and his descriptions of sex bordered on the pornographic, the book had created a minor sensation. As few people knew more about tribal life in Africa than Marcel Colbert, the Princesse hoped that a meeting between the two men might provide a stimulating conversation centrepiece for her dinner and her soirée that evening.

The remaining guests at dinner were an author and his wife and a retired general. Ferdinand Couvier was a member of the Académie française, and his books on ancient history were well-regarded, although their sales were modest. General Charles Dumont, one of the few heroes of the war with Germany in 1870, was a widower, now very old, and a close friend of the Princesse, who often invited him to act as host at her dinner parties.

The conversation at dinner was not as stimulating as the Princesse had no doubt hoped. Professor Kastrup contributed little, appearing shy and ill at ease, even though his command of French was impressive. Like many authors, he was surprisingly inarticulate, as though only the pen and not the tongue could be the medium for his fluency with words. Marcel Colbert did what he could to make up for the Dane's reticence, trying to entertain the party with stories of his travels in Africa, but there was no interplay between the two men, no witty arguments, no sparkle. Nor was there any mention of snakes, but then Gautier had not really expected that there would be.

If Princesse Hélène was disappointed, she was too accomplished a hostess to show it. Her popularity and the reputation of her salon had been built on her personality. When she had first come to live in Paris more than thirty years previously, she had been regarded as an upstart and ignored. Although she used the title of *princesse*, people felt she was not entitled to it, since she had been born, to put it politely, on the wrong side of the blanket, her father one of Napoléon's brothers whom he had placed on the thrones of Europe, her mother's name mercifully hidden in obscurity. In a short time, however, Parisians had decided that she was worth cultivating, not only for her wealth, although that was an asset, but for her charm, her eccentricity and her candour.

'If it was not for my uncle,' she would say, 'I would be selling oranges in the streets of Ajaccio.'

At dinner that evening, aware that her guests were losing interest in tales of Africa, she tried to steer the conversation into less intellectually strenuous topics. 'Have you heard,' she asked the others, 'that Madame de Fleurie is moving out of Paris to live in Neuilly?'

'She must be mad!' Madame Colbert exclaimed. 'Why on earth is she moving?'

'For the sake of her Afghan hounds. She believes it is cruel to keep dogs in a Paris apartment. In Neuilly she will be able to take the two monsters for long walks.'

'She will lose all her friends,' Catriona Becker commented. 'No one will go all the way to Neuilly to call on her. She is committing social suicide.'

'Poor fellow!' General Dumont said suddenly. 'But who can blame him? London is a frightful place; a desert of culture, uncivilized, full of perverts and cut-throats.'

Everyone at the table looked at the General in astonishment. He had scarcely spoken at all during dinner. Gautier remembered then that the man was very deaf, even though he attempted to conceal his deafness. Clearly he must have heard the one word 'suicide' mentioned and assumed that the conversation was about the death of the French Ambassador in London.

'Quite so,' the Princesse said. She was too kind to embarrass the General by pointing out his gaffe.

Gautier felt he should help her. 'Did I not read that not long ago the Ambassador came to Paris for consultations?'

'That was the official reason for his visit,' Princesse Hélène replied bluntly, 'but we have to face the truth, which is that he came here to see his wife; to implore her to go and live with him in London.'

61

'Had they been living apart?' Colbert asked. 'I did not know there had been trouble between them.'

'Not everyone in Paris knows, for it was only a very recent and minor scandal. You were probably abroad when she left him.'

'Didn't you know of this?' Colbert asked his wife, truculently accusing her of keeping the story from him. 'You and Elizabeth Deslandes have always been close friends.'

'I did hear they had separated, but I felt it would have been undiplomatic to ask her about it.' Madame Colbert seemed uncomfortable at having been asked the question.

'One can only feel sorry for their son,' the General said. 'This is bound to damage his military career.'

'He has already resigned his commission,' Princesse Hélène said. 'Some weeks ago when the trouble between his parents started. He is living at home with his mother now, which will probably not please him. Luc was devoted to his father but, like many army officers, he is inclined to treat women with a haughty indifference.'

His Excellency Ambassador Eugène Deslandes, Gautier learned, had left a son and two daughters. The daughters were both married, one to an Italian diplomat, the other to a brilliant young professor in Heidelberg. Luc, the son, was in his thirties, and had been serving in one of France's artillery regiments.

'Obviously, Madame Deslandes will not be coming to your soirée this evening,' Madame Colbert said. 'You were expecting her, were you not, Princesse?'

'Yes, and Luc as well, but I had a *petit bleu* from Madame Deslandes this morning, giving their excuses. Poor Luc is desolate! He adored his father.'

Gautier noticed that Madame Becker had said nothing at all during the conversation about the French Ambassador's death. More than that, she seemed to be showing no interest in it, keeping her eyes averted from the speakers almost ostentatiously, as though she had no wish to become involved in the discussion. He wondered why. Could it be that her reticence and the obvious unease of Madame Colbert were in some way related? He dismissed the idea as just a policeman's habitual suspicion.

After dinner, the ladies left the dining-room, leaving the men to enjoy a glass of Cognac and a cigar. When they had gone, General Dumont said, 'This is a dreadful business about poor Deslandes!'

'Are we to assume that he killed himself because his wife left him?' Couvier asked.

'It would seem so. People say she is having an affair with another man here and refused to leave Paris. Of course the scandal would have made his position in London untenable.'

'He was too soft with her,' Colbert said. He was a powerful, muscular man and one could imagine him bullying any primitive tribesmen who confronted him in Africa. 'He should have discovered who this lover was, given him a good thrashing and compelled his wife to go with him to London.'

'I doubt whether she would have responded to compulsion,' Couvier said. He was known for his liberal views. 'I rather suspect that what she has done is by way of being a rebellion, and perhaps one that is overdue.'

'A rebellion? Against what?'

'Against male domination. Elizabeth married into a military family, where she was expected always to comply with a masculine code of behaviour. I have known her for many years and, in my view, she has always been afraid of her husband and to a lesser extent of her son.'

The other men were not disposed to argue with this view. As the conversation rumbled on, Gautier might have felt uncomfortable, but he realized that no one in the room could have known that his wife too had left him.

Presently, the ladies returned, and they all went to the salon where the guests for the soirée would soon be arriving. Like most of the drawing-rooms of *le monde* in Paris, the room seemed overcrowded even before anyone entered it. Paintings, some classical, some banal, were hung on all four walls. Every table was crowded with ornaments and mementoes: silver boxes, Venetian glass vases, framed photographs, plastic busts of famous composers, a model of the Eiffel Tower and even picture postcards, including one of Ajaccio, where the Princesse might now have been selling oranges. Gautier was disappointed to find the salon so conventional, with no signs of Princesse Hélène's notorious eccentricity. As all Paris knew, in her boudoir she kept two pet monkeys, a solid gold bicycle, a satin-lined coffin waiting for her last repose and a life-sized sculpture of herself in the nude, which she would dress with a bathing costume when visitors were expected.

While the Princesse was by the door receiving the guests, Gautier found himself alone with Catriona Becker. 'I read about Ambassador Deslandes's death in the newspapers today,' he told her. 'Is it true that the Ambassador's wife refused to live with him in London?'

'Yes. Madame Deslandes says she could not bear to be away from her lover,' Catriona Becker replied. Then she added with obvious irritation, 'It's ridiculous! A woman of her age!'

'How old is she?'

'More than fifty.'

'And the man is younger than she?'

'Much younger.'

Gautier sensed that Catriona Becker did not like talking about Madame Deslandes and her lover, not through embarrassment, but because for some reason the subject irritated her. She was spared further irritation, for at that point Princesse Hélène began taking her Danish guest round the room and introducing him to the company. Catriona Becker and he found themselves in a small group listening to Henning Kastrup as he answered questions about his book, his views on life in Paris and the political situation.

The soirée was not a success. Kastrup had nothing amusing or witty to say, and guests who had come expecting to hear salacious explanations of his theories on primitive sex were only given a boring academic lecture. The Princesse, though, was an experienced hostess and had alternative entertainment for them ready in reserve.

Among her invitees to the soirée was a talented young pianist who not long previously had won the Prix de Rome, and he was persuaded without too much difficulty to perform for the company. The pieces he chose to play were by Debussy, a choice which gave the other guests a subject for titillating gossip. Only a short time ago, Debussy had abandoned his attractive and devoted young wife to elope with the wealthy, middle-aged mother of one of his pianoforte pupils. His wife had then tried to kill herself and the resulting scandal had still not subsided.

While the pianist was playing, Gautier noticed, standing among a group on the far side of the room, the Comte de Chartres and his wife Maria. When she was younger, the Comtesse had been recognized to be one of the loveliest women in Paris and now, in her thirties, she still retained much of her dark, Latin beauty. Gautier remembered Courtrand saying that she had been unfaithful to her husband again since her liaison with the Prince of Wales. Evidently, the affair was not notorious enough to prevent her escorting her husband to social events. Either the Comte did not appear to notice that Gautier was at the soirée that evening, or he was deliberately ignoring him.

Now that she had put the thoughts of the Ambassador's suicide and his wife's lover out of her mind, Catriona Becker was enjoying the evening. Clearly she had many friends who enjoyed her company, her welcoming manner and her easy charm. Comtesse Maria de Chartres must have been one of her friends, for at one point in the evening she left Gautier and crossed the room to speak to her. The two women left the room together for a short time, and when Catriona returned she appeared thoughtful. The mood did not last, though, and soon she was laughing and chatting with the other guests again.

When they were being driven in her carriage back to her apartment, Gautier asked her, 'How well do you know the Comtesse de Chartres?'

'Very well. Maria and I are about the same age. Why do you ask?'

'The Comte has been acting foolishly. I was obliged to warn him about his behaviour.'

'Good heavens! When was that?'

Gautier could see no harm in telling Catriona of the incident in the Moulin Rouge. It was quite likely that the story would appear in one of the newspapers, if indeed it had not been published already.

'How stupid of Edmond! He is attacking the wrong man.'

'So I understand.'

'What have you heard?' Catriona asked at once.

'That the Comtesse has another more recent lover.'

'I know nothing about that.'

'They say all Paris is talking about it. If it is true, surely you as a good friend of hers would know?'

Catriona did not answer the question. Instead, she was silent for a time, and one sensed that she was facing conflicting impulses, a reluctance to confide in Gautier and a feeling that perhaps he might be the only person who could help her. Her next remark was unexpected.

'You said earlier that you had little experience of blackmail.'

'That's true.'

'Even so, what advice would you give to anyone who was being blackmailed?'

'To inform the police as soon as possible.'

'In spite of the consequences? Shame? Humiliation?'

'Blackmailers do not always carry out their threats. And in many cases, the police are able to prevent them doing so.'

Catriona sighed. 'If only one could rely on that!'

Gautier hesitated, thinking how he could best phrase the question he was going to ask. He decided that there was no point in being delicate. 'Forgive me for asking, Madame, but is it the Comtesse de Chartres who is being blackmailed? Or is it you?'

'We both are.'

'By whom?'

'I cannot tell you that; not yet anyway.'

Gautier did not press for an answer. He knew now that what he had suspected was true. The Prefect of Police had manoeuvred him into a position in which he would be expected to help Madame Becker, to extricate her from her difficulties. The manoeuvre had been executed with finesse and subtlety, and he would be expected to respond with tact. What Catriona said next confirmed his decision.

'Let us make that the subject for our next English lesson.' Her laugh was forced, but not painfully so. 'Shall we meet tomorrow evening at the same time?'

Chapter 7

As he crossed Pont Neuf, heading for the Left Bank and the Paris home of the deceased French Ambassador, Gautier resolved that he would not allow the day's inauspicious start to discourage him. On arriving at the Quai des Orfèvres that morning, he had discovered that in his absence Courtrand had been interfering with all the criminal investigations which the Sûreté was carrying out. As a general rule, the Director General took almost no interest in the day-to-day work of his department. The role he preferred was representing the Sûreté on State and ceremonial occasions and at Government meetings, where he could take credit for its successes and its growing prestige. From time to time, though, usually when his wife was being difficult at home, he decided that he must demonstrate his authority and his powers of leadership. This took the form of sending for the dossiers of cases under investigation, examining the deployment of staff, changing work schedules and generally creating disorder.

That morning, having learned that Gautier had assigned police officers to provide Armand de Périgord a measure of protection, he had immediately cancelled the operation. What he had done was really no more than a minor irritation. Gautier himself had begun to question whether the employment of policemen to guard de Périgord was justified. He was by no means convinced that the man's life really was in danger. Putting a snake in his bed might have been just a practical joke by one of his friends which had misfired. In spite of these doubts, Gautier had been ready to provide him with police protection, at least for a little longer, because he had a feeling, just intuition one might say, that the incident of the snake was part of a larger plot, as yet undefined, and that there might be more violence to come.

Another cause for the niggling irritation he felt was the assignment he had been given that morning. The previous evening, the Sûreté had received a telegram from the Metropolitan Police in London, who were carrying out an enquiry into the death of the French Ambassador. They were asking the Sûreté to interview the dead man's widow and family in Paris about his death. Although it appeared fairly certain that the Ambassador had shot himself, he had left no suicide note. Questions would be asked at the inquest. Had the dead man given his family any reason for believing that he might kill himself? Was he in financial difficulties? Had he seemed depressed on his recent visit to Paris?

When he had been shown the telegram, Courtrand had at once handed it to Gautier. 'This must be one for you, Gautier,' he had said sarcastically. 'You are our expert on the English.' He did not approve of Gautier's English lessons, nor of the encouragement which the Prefect of Police had given him to take them.

Given the circumstances of the Ambassador's death, official enquiries had to be made, but Gautier wished it was not he who had to make them. Intruding on a family's grief after a bereavement was always embarrassing and, in this case, if, as Princesse Hélène had suggested the previous evening, the reason for the Ambassador's suicide had been his wife's infidelity, an interview with her would be more than usually painful.

The Ambassador's house was in Rue Jacob, on the fringe of Faubourg St Germain, and it was larger than one might have expected. Members of the diplomatic corps spent so little time in their own countries, that to maintain a large establishment was seldom justified. Before leaving the Sûreté, Gautier had found out what he could about Ambassador Deslandes from the diplomatic lists and other official records. No obituary of him had yet been published in the newspapers, but that could be expected in a day or so.

Eugène Deslandes had come of a military family, which for generations had given loyal service to France. The younger son of a general, he had not followed his father and elder brother into the army, but had chosen a diplomat's career. The list of his appointments showed that the decision had been a sound one, for he had been stationed in only the more desirable consulates and embassies, finishing with what was accepted to be the post which carried the most prestige, that of Ambassador in London. One might assume that Deslandes must have had money of his own, for to enter the diplomatic service without a private income would be unthinkable, but his wife's wealth must have been a great help to him and enabled them to maintain the house in Rue Jacob.

Elizabeth Deslandes was the only daughter of a businessman in Bordeaux who, in addition to interests in shipping, owned extensive vineyards, including a château associated with one of the best known of the Grand Cru wines. He had been one of the first wine growers to exploit the increasing interest of the British and the Americans in the great wines of France.

The door of the house in Rue Jacob was opened to Gautier by a manservant, who seemed surprised that anyone should be calling on a family in mourning. When Gautier explained who he was, the man let him into the house, took his visiting card and went off to find out whether his mistress would see him. Presently, he returned and ushered him into the drawing-room, where he was to wait. While he was waiting, Gautier looked round the room, which was furnished in much the same style as the salon of Princesse Hélène. Among the jumbled disorder, though, one could see ornaments and mementoes which had been acquired during the Ambassador's service overseas; a small brass Buddha, carved elephants' tusks, boxes inlaid with mother of pearl, a bullfighter's sword. On one wall hung a portrait in oils of a woman, the work,

Gautier suspected, of one of the established artists of the time, Bouguereau, perhaps.

The woman in the portrait, Gautier supposed, must be the Ambassador's wife, painted when she was younger. One could not call it a beautiful face. Although, no doubt, the artist had done his best to flatter his sitter, he had not been able to conceal the features, the eyes set too close together, the long nose and teeth that were too large for the mouth. Gautier could not help feeling that it would have been kinder to the woman not to have had a portrait commissioned, or at least not to have hung it in such a prominent position.

When Madame Deslandes arrived, he could not be sure if the portrait was one of her, for she was wearing a veil. Many Frenchwomen still wore veils at Mass or at funerals, or in public when convention demanded that they should be in mourning.

'Madame,' Gautier began, 'allow me to offer you my condolences and those of the Sûreté.' Madame Deslandes nodded, sat down and pointed in the direction of a chair to tell Gautier he should do so too. He continued, 'I must apologize most sincerely for intruding on your privacy at a time of grief. Regrettably, there are certain formalities which the law requires us to observe.'

'I understand, Inspector, that you are making enquiries concerning my husband's death.' Madame Deslandes's voice was controlled, with no sign of emotion.

'Not on our own account, Madame. The police in London have asked us to assist them.'

'Are they not satisfied then that my husband killed himself?' Madame Deslandes asked with no more than the faintest touch of irony.

'No doubt they are, but even so they are required by law to try and find out why he did so. An inquest will be held, you understand.'

'I understand. They need evidence as to his mental state. They would prefer to believe that he was, for the time at least, out of his mind.'

Madame Deslandes sighed. One could not be sure

whether it was a sigh of regret or exasperation. 'Inspector Gautier,' she said, 'I am sure you already know the circumstances which led to my husband's death. You know that we were living apart.'

'I had heard so, Madame.'

'Precisely! The matter was discussed in the home of Princesse Hélène last evening where you were one of the guests at dinner.' Madame Deslandes paused, and then she explained, 'Madame Colbert telephoned me this morning.'

'Your husband came back to Paris not long ago. Did you see him during his visit?'

'Of course.'

'And how was his manner? Did he behave normally?'

Madame Deslandes shook her head, not in answer to the question but as though the memory of her husband's behaviour still irritated her. 'Inspector, my husband was a sensitive, highly strung man. Had he not been so he would have joined the army. As it was, all his life he needed constant reassurance; reassurance that people did not hate him, that they were not conspiring against him. My role in our years together was to provide that reassurance. Recently, he was unable to accept that our married life had run its course. He was devastated. Another man might have seen my leaving him as a blow to his vanity, but for Eugène it was far worse. The whole fabric of his personality, his pride, his self-confidence, seemed to collapse. Do you think you could explain that to your colleagues in London?'

'I will certainly tell them what you have told me, Madame,' Gautier replied.

As he was speaking, the door from the hallway into the drawing-room was flung open. For a moment, Gautier was startled, thinking that the man who stood in the entrance staring at him was the Prefect of Police. Then he realized that, though similar in looks and in build, the man was a good deal younger than the Prefect. He was also clearly very angry.

'Luc, *chéri*,' Madame Deslandes said to him, 'this is

Chief Inspector Gautier from the Sûreté. He is here about Papa.'

'This is monstrous!' Luc Deslandes shouted at Gautier. 'How dare you?'

'Monsieur?' Gautier realized that the manservant who had let him into the house must have told Madame Deslandes's son that he was there.

'Have you no sense of propriety? No humanity? My father's body is scarcely cold and you come to invade my mother's grief and torture her with questions!'

'Calm yourself, Luc.'

'Your behaviour is intolerable! Your Director General will hear of this.'

'I would rather answer Inspector Gautier's questions here at home in Paris than before the inquisitive eyes of Londoners at an inquest,' his mother said.

Luc Deslandes ranted on a little longer before calming down. His indignation, it seemed to Gautier, was largely bluster, a show put on by a dutiful son protective of his mother. When he was allowed to, Gautier asked Madame Deslandes a few more questions, without learning anything of any significance. Then he turned to her son.

'And you, Monsieur? Can you think of any reason why your father should have wished to take his own life?'

'Me? Why should I know?' Luc immediately seemed to go on the defensive.

'Did you not see him on his recent visit to Paris?'

'No.'

'But Luc, *chéri*—' Madame began, and then checked herself.

'I was away from home and my father had to return to London sooner than he had expected.' Deslandes did not look at his mother when he was speaking, and Gautier suspected that he must be lying.

'Your father had no financial difficulties, I suppose?'

'On the contrary, not long ago he inherited a substantial legacy when his mother died.'

'And no problems in his diplomatic career?'

'None. The Ministry for Foreign Affairs will tell you

what an able and popular ambassador he had proved himself to be.'

'In that case, I need trouble you no further, Monsieur, Madame.'

Gautier could see no point in prolonging his visit. He would report what he had learned to London and the police there would decide what further action they might wish to take. The breakdown of the Deslandes's marriage might be mentioned at the inquest, but he doubted it. In England, as in France, the authorities were solicitous of the feelings of well-connected or wealthy people and would be doubly so in the case of a foreign diplomat's family.

In the hallway outside the drawing-room, the manservant who had admitted him to the house was waiting to show him out. As the man opened the front door, they saw that another visitor, a woman, was approaching the house. As she drew near, Gautier saw that it was the Comtesse de Chartres. Although she and Gautier had never formally met, he thought it was likely that she knew who he was. As they passed each other, she looked at him, a look full of interest, which lingered, as though it might turn into a smile. Then, remembering perhaps that she was entering a house of bereavement, she nodded abruptly and hurried into the house.

That afternoon, the Sûreté had one of those strokes of good fortune which often seem to come to the aid of police in their work. As Gautier knew, luck was almost always a factor in any successful criminal investigation. The previous day, a man named Buisson had been found dead in a small hotel in the 12th *Arrondissement*. His death had been unspectacular, not entirely accidental, for he had been carried off by apoplexy in the arms of a young lady of the streets. Like many men, Buisson had been a creature of habit, visiting the same hotel every Tuesday and Friday in the late afternoon, always at the same time though not always with the same girl. Over the years, he had become a friend of the hotel's owner, but when the police had been called and they searched

74

his pockets, they found he was carrying a visiting card printed with the name of Laborde and giving an address in Montparnasse.

That might have seemed to be of little consequence, but the policeman who found the card had a good memory and recalled that the name Laborde was on a list of people whom the Sûreté wished to trace, which had been circulated only that day to the police *commissariats* of every *arrondissement*. It had not taken long to establish that Buisson was a jobbing printer with a small business near Rue Réaumur, where he printed visiting cards, wedding invitations, admission tickets, leaflets and any other items too small to be of interest to a larger firm. An officer from the Sûreté was sent to Buisson's premises, where he found copies of every visiting card that had been printed there, kept for reference purposes in the event of repeat orders. It became clear that Buisson had been carrying the Laborde card in a clumsy and futile attempt to conceal his identity when he went whoring. The address given on the card proved to be false; not that of an apartment but of a florist's shop. Buisson had an assistant who remembered that they had printed quantities of two cards for Laborde, one with the Montparnasse address and one with the name and address of a firm of musical instrument manufacturers. Enquiries showed that there was no such firm in Paris.

As soon as Gautier had been told about the cards, he sent for the officer who had been to Buisson's premises and asked him, 'Did the assistant give a description of Laborde?'

'Apparently he never saw Laborde, Chief Inspector. Buisson must have taken the order for the cards when the assistant was not there. He remembers though that the two packets of cards were collected for Laborde by a coachman.'

'A coachman?'

'That would not be unusual. Having placed an order and paid for the work, customers frequently send a servant to collect it.'

'Did the assistant describe this coachman?'

The policeman pulled a face. 'Not really. He's only a boy and not very bright. All he could say was that the coachman was dressed in brown livery and carried a whip. We were lucky to get anything specific out of him at all.'

Soon after the officer had left Gautier's office, Surat arrived to report on the enquiries which he had made among the staff of the Hôtel Meurice the previous evening. He told Gautier gloomily that his efforts had not been particularly fruitful.

'Did you not learn anything?' Gautier asked him.

'A waiter remembers that the workman carrying the plumber's tools borrowed a passkey from a chambermaid who was working on the same floor as de Périgord's suite. The man gave the key back to her a couple of minutes later.'

'So he had the key long enough to pick up the French horn case from Goesler's suite, take it to de Périgord's bedroom and release the snake into his bed?'

'The waiter believes he may have seen the man somewhere before.'

'In the hotel?'

'He doesn't think it was in the hotel. Certainly, the man is not on the hotel's staff. The Meurice has its own team of men to look after maintenance: plumbers, carpenters, electricians.'

'No,' Gautier agreed, 'the man would not be on the staff, but he seems to have known his way about the hotel and no one recognized him as an impostor.'

'If this Laborde was hired to kill Monsieur de Périgord,' Surat said, 'and if he comes from outside Paris, he will probably have left the city by now.'

'I doubt it. He hasn't accomplished what he was hired to do and so will not have been paid.'

'If he has a coachman of his own, he must be a man of substance.'

'Possibly. On the other hand, perhaps he is a coachman himself.'

The idea had come to Gautier suddenly, and he sensed at once that he was right. A coachman in the employ of a wealthy family in Paris would certainly know the Hôtel Meurice. He would have driven members of the family there, might have been kept waiting at the hotel and chatted with the staff, might even have drunk with them in the local bistro.

'Go and see your waiter friend again,' he told Surat. 'Ask him if the man he saw carrying the plumber's tools might not in fact have been a coachman. A coachman whom he had seen working for guests at the hotel, a coachman dressed in brown livery.'

'By the way,' Surat said, 'as I was leaving the Meurice, the concierge, Rodier, stopped me. He asked me to tell you that he has seen Monsieur Montbrun again.'

'In the hotel?'

'No, by the entrance, talking to one of the porters. When Rodier warned de Périgord that the man was there, he left the hotel by the back way.'

Chapter 8

'The correct spelling of the name is S.T.E.W.A.R.T.,' Catriona Becker said, 'but because the letter "W" does not exist in the French alphabet, the spelling was changed for the sake of the French to S.T.U.A.R.T. One finds both versions in Scotland now.'

As part of his second French lesson, she was telling Gautier of the long and close ties between her country and France, of the Auld Alliance against the common enemy, England. She was speaking in English, slowly so that Gautier could understand, and from time to time she would draw a comment or a remark from him with questions.

After a time, as she had done on his previous visit, the Scottish maid brought in a decanter of whisky and two glasses. Catriona took the opportunity to switch the lesson to a discussion of Scotch. The whisky they were drinking, she told him, came from the Glenlivet distillery. The valley of the River Livet, only a short distance from where she had been born, was famous for its whisky, and at one time more than two hundred small distilleries could be found there, all operating illegally.

Catriona was a natural teacher, and as she gradually broke down Gautier's reticence, he found himself enjoying the lesson. Even so, he was aware that it was only a device, contrived by the Prefect of Police to bring him and Madame Becker together. If he were to help her over the threat of blackmail which she faced, then the sooner she told him about it the better.

So when she broke off the lesson to pour the whisky

78

for them, he told her, 'I called on the widow of the French Ambassador this morning, in an official capacity.'

Catriona laughed. 'That was a subtle question, was it not? I can see that you're impatient to hear about my blackmailer.'

'Yes, but not just through curiosity. I may be able to help you.'

'I wonder where I should begin.'

'You could tell me who it is that is blackmailing you.'

'That's the problem. I have no idea who it is. The threats and demands for money which I have received have all been anonymous.'

'Demands? There has been more than one, then?'

'Yes. Little notes delivered to the house at night. Just handed in to the concierge without any explanation. I destroyed the first one, threw it away, believing it was just a silly practical joke by one of my friends.'

'What happened then?'

'A second note arrived. It was much harsher than the first, warning me not to ignore it and demanding a payment of fifty thousand francs.'

'Did you keep this second note?'

'Yes.'

A book lay on the table beside her chair and from it Catriona drew a half-sheet of paper which had been tucked inside. The blackmail note was neatly written in block capitals on paper which looked as though it may have been torn out of a pad.

MADAME,

SINCE YOU HAVE IGNORED MY PREVIOUS INSTRUCTIONS, I AM FORCED TO WRITE TO YOU AGAIN, AND THIS TIME YOU WOULD BE FOOLHARDY IF YOU DO NOT TAKE HEED OF WHAT I SAY. YOUR VISITS TO RUE DES MOINES ARE WELL-ILLUSTRATED, AND UNLESS YOU MAKE AN IMMEDIATE PAYMENT OF 50,000 FRANCS, FOLLOWING THE SAME DIRECTIONS AS WERE GIVEN TO YOU PREVIOUSLY, ALL THE MATERIAL WILL BE FORWARDED TO PITTSBURGH.

79

'How long ago did you receive this?' Gautier asked Catriona.

'About four weeks.'

'And you have done nothing?'

'Oh yes. I paid the money.'

Gautier shook his head reproachfully. 'That was very unwise, Madame.'

'I realize that now. Only two days ago this arrived.'

She drew another sheet of paper from the book in her hands. The message written on it was briefer than in the first demand. Catriona read it out to him. 'You must pay a further thirty thousand francs if you wish your indiscretions to remain a secret. Follow the same instructions as before.'

'The implication of the threat, I assume,' Gautier said, 'is that unless you pay the money, evidence of your indiscretions will be sent to the American gentleman whom you plan to marry.'

The mention of her fiancé had a devastating effect on Catriona. Her composure seemed to disintegrate. No one could deny that she was an attractive woman, but Gautier realized now that it was her vivacity and effervescent charm which made her face appear more than attractive, lovely even. Now with despair in her eyes, she seemed weary and plain.

'If Wayne were to find out,' she said helplessly, 'that would be the end of our marriage. He would never condone what I did.'

'This indiscretion involved another man, one supposes.'

'Yes. I was mad, crazy! I can see that now. You could blame boredom, loneliness. It was an adventure, nothing more, and I thought no one could possibly find out.'

Gautier knew that Rue des Moines was a small street near Porte de Clichy. It was a district of no importance, but he supposed there might be hotels there. Catriona seemed reluctant to tell him exactly what indiscretions she had committed, so he decided to essay a guess.

'This Rue des Moines? Did you allow a man to take you to a hotel there?' he asked her bluntly.

80

'An *hôtel-de-rendezvous*? How can you possibly think that? I am not a *cocotte*,' Catriona said indignantly. 'No, I simply went to his *garçonnière*.'

'Why not tell me about it?'

'It began harmlessly enough.'

Slowly the story emerged. Catriona had taken a little too much wine at a lunch party and had been persuaded by the man, a fellow guest, to meet him at his apartment later the same afternoon. There had been no question of their making love there, for she had known the man for some time and he had never shown any romantic interest in her. At the apartment, they had drunk champagne together and she had allowed him to photograph her, that was all.

Photography had become a fashionable craze in Paris society. Professional photographers charged huge fees for studio portraits of wealthy ladies and the great *cocottes*, while amateurs tried to imitate them by photographing their relatives and friends. Their efforts were often surprisingly competent technically, but spoilt by their staging, with the sitters wearing historical costumes and posing against elaborate, allegorical backgrounds.

'Your visit to this man's apartment appears to have been innocent enough,' Gautier agreed, 'and it is hard to understand how it could be used as a reason for blackmail.'

'Wayne would be horrified if he learnt that I had gone to a man's apartment, unchaperoned and alone.'

'How could anyone prove you had been there?'

'The concierge of the building would have seen me arrive.'

'Concierges do not spy on their tenants. They have to be discreet or they would lose their positions.'

'Then there are the photographs which my friend took of me. Anyone would recognize the room where they were taken.' Catriona hesitated before she added, 'The décor is very distinctive. The paintings hanging on the walls are, shall we say, highly suggestive.'

Her hesitation made Gautier wonder whether Catriona

was telling him the whole truth. Could it be that she had allowed herself to be photographed naked? Two years previously, Liane de Pougy, one of the best known *cocottes* in Paris – the great horizontals as they were facetiously called – had been photographed in the nude. Within weeks, copies of the photographs were being circulated among members of the Jockey Club. The scandal had done no damage to Liane de Pougy's social position, for she had none. Instead, they had made her even more desirable to the *roués* of Paris. One admirer was even said to have paid a hundred thousand francs simply to see her naked. Gautier decided, though, that he would keep his suspicions to himself. Catriona had already shown signs of having a quick temper.

'Who has seen these photographs?'

'That's just it. My friend took more than one. He sent me one, which I immediately destroyed. Then he told me that he had mislaid the others. He believes they may have been stolen.'

'Have you thought that it might be your friend himself who is blackmailing you? That the visit to his apartment, the photographs, were all part of a plot to make you vulnerable to blackmail?'

'That's absurd! A preposterous suggestion. The man is a friend; he has a position in society. Besides, he has no reason to resort to blackmail. He's a wealthy man.'

'Do I know him?'

'I cannot possibly tell you his name.'

'I regret that I must insist that you do, Madame.' Gautier was growing irritated. Through no choice of his own, he had been involved in what appeared more and more to be just a foolish and slightly sordid escapade of a young woman who should have known better. 'If you do not tell me the name of this man, I shall inform the Prefect of Police that I can do nothing to help you in this affair.'

'Oh, very well,' Catriona said petulantly. 'But I rely on your discretion. It was Monsieur Armand de Périgord.'

*

'You can have no idea how much I enjoy having dinner at home,' Catriona told Gautier. Then she added, 'Tête-à-tête, I mean.'

Her remark was neither coy nor flirtatious, merely a statement of her views, intended to show perhaps that the frivolity of life in society did not really appeal to her. Gautier had agreed to stay on and dine with her in her apartment, but only with misgivings. He had at first declined her invitation, but Catriona had pressed him to stay with a surprising persistence. Finally, he had given in, partly because he had further questions to ask her. Another reason was that the alternative, to dine alone in some café or bistro as he did on most evenings, was even less appealing.

'Do you often entertain at home?' he asked her.

'Very seldom now. When my husband was alive we frequently did.' Their meal had been served by the Scottish maid. 'Now, as you can see, I do not have enough servants to do more than a lunch or dinner for one or two intimate friends.'

'Is the Comtesse de Chartres one of them?'

'She is now. We have become close friends.'

'Because you are both being blackmailed?'

'That may have been what brought us together.' Catriona did not appear to mind the directness of his questions.

'And how did the Comtesse fall from grace?'

Catriona looked at him sharply, but restrained the reply she may have wished to make. 'You may think it strange, but the circumstances of her indiscreet behaviour were very similar to mine. She too went unchaperoned to a man's apartment.'

'The same man?'

'Yes, but there is nothing remarkable about that. He has been a good friend to her as well.'

'And she too allowed him to photograph her?'

'I cannot say. She may have done, for she visited his *garçonnière* more than once.'

'Forgive my frankness, but were they lovers?'

'I am certain they were not.'

'And has she also complied with the blackmailer's demands?'

'Yes. Like me, she gave him fifty thousand. Now she has been asked for more.'

The story he was being told seemed to Gautier bizarre. He knew that many married women in Paris society were frivolous and spoilt. With too much time on their hands, they frequently looked for an escape from boredom in clandestine affairs with men. That was understandable, particularly since all too often they were aware that their husbands were being unfaithful, either with mistresses they had installed in apartments or with well-known *cocottes*. What Gautier found hard to understand was how Armand de Périgord had been able to persuade two attractive and wealthy women to visit his apartment in such circumstances, when they should have realized that they were exposing themselves to the danger of scandal, if not of blackmail. He could not help wondering how many other women might have been trapped into similar indiscretions.

'You told me earlier that de Périgord was to have escorted you to Princesse Hélène's soirée,' he said to Catriona, 'but that he was not able to go.'

'That was not strictly true. I decided it would be imprudent for us to be seen together.'

'Is that the reason, or was it because you had discovered that he was seeing another woman?'

The question displeased Catriona, and her resentment showed in the brusque tone of her reply. 'That is not the reason, but if you must know, he has.'

'Could it be the Ambassador's wife?'

'Now I know why the Prefect of Police suggested you might be able to help me. You're too clever by half, Inspector, as the English would say. Yes, it is Madame Deslandes.'

Gautier could now see an inevitability in Madame Becker's replies to his questions and in the questions themselves. It was as though they were all part of a game, a game which, at another time, he might have found interesting to watch, but in which he was now, reluctantly, a player. No one was going to tell him the rules of the game, so he would be obliged to work them out for himself.

'Monsieur de Périgord appears to have a surprising success with women,' he observed drily, 'for one who is commonly supposed to be a pederast.'

'That may be the reason for his success. Because men believe he is a *pédé*, they do not object when he pays attention to their wives.'

'And is he a *pédé*?'

'How would I know? At one time I thought he might be, because he is always on the defensive. Have you noticed how *pédés* seem to believe that the whole world hates them? Armand seems to be convinced that his life is in danger.'

'From whom?'

'Who knows? I find him hard to understand. He pays women compliments, flirts with them outrageously, kisses them in an avuncular way, but I have never heard that he has taken one to bed; at least not until now.'

'You mean the Ambassador's wife?'

'She is boasting that she is his mistress, but I would need to see them in bed before I believed that.'

'It is not unknown for men to have sexual relations with a woman, father her children, at the same time as he is furtively visiting homosexual brothels.'

'I find that disgusting!'

They had finished dinner and Gautier followed her into the drawing-room, where the Scottish maid served them a glass of Cognac. Catriona evidently believed she had told him as much as he needed to know about the blackmail threats she had received, and they began discussing the manners of society in France and its attitude to homosexuals. Until a few years ago, homosexuals had been tolerated, particularly if they were men of talent, but since the disgrace of Oscar Wilde, attitudes had hardened. People also believed that homosexuality was undermining the virility of Frenchmen and that it must be eliminated if the nation were to overcome the Germans in the war of revenge which many thought was inevitable. So now homosexuals in France did their best to conceal their predilections. In spite of her claim that she found male brothels disgusting, Catriona seemed able to discuss the question dispassionately and with intelligence.

When the time came for Gautier to leave, he remembered that there was one more question he should ask her. 'Does Armand de Périgord know that you are being blackmailed?'

'Yes. I had not wished to tell him, but then I thought he might be able to guess who the blackmailer might be. He was furious when I told him; threatened that he would find who was responsible and kill him.'

'Did he encourage you to pay the demands?'

'Not at first, but then he agreed it was the only prudent course.'

'Did he offer to pay? You say he is a wealthy man.'

Catriona's hesitation before replying was only fleeting. 'He did, of course, but I would not allow it.'

After leaving, Gautier crossed Boulevard Haussmann and walked past the Madeleine, heading for Place de la Concorde. His meeting with Catriona had left him restless and dissatisfied. His mood as he was listening to what she said, had alternated between scepticism and irritation; scepticism because much of what she was telling him seemed highly implausible, irritation because he was being asked to extricate her from difficulties of her own making.

It was well past midnight, but even so he decided he would drop in at Sûreté headquarters, as he often did after dining alone in some nearby café. He had half persuaded himself that his mind worked better late at night, enabling him to sift and analyse more clearly the problems which the day had brought. His real motive was a hope that at the Sûreté he would find some reason for postponing his return to an empty apartment. That evening when he arrived he went to see the inspector on night duty.

'Has anything happened to spoil my evening?' he asked him flippantly.

'That depends on what view you take. You know this character Armand de Périgord, who was being given police protection until Courtrand cancelled it this morning?'

'What about him?'

'He was killed not long ago when a bomb exploded in his carriage as he was driving through the Bois de Boulogne.'

Chapter 9

Armand de Périgord had been killed as he was being driven home after dining with friends in a restaurant. By the time an ambulance had arrived in the Bois de Boulogne, he was dead, and so was the coachman who had been driving him. The two horses pulling the carriage had been badly mutilated by the explosion of the bomb and both had had to be destroyed.

Early the following morning, a fiacre took Gautier out to the Bois de Boulogne. What was left of the carriage still lay in one of the lanes leading away from the Pré Catalan towards Paris. The force of the explosion had completely wrecked the *calèche*. Only one of its four wheels was intact. The other three, the side panels and the coachman's seat at the front were in splinters. De Périgord's body and that of the coachman had been taken by ambulance to the mortuary, but those of the horses lay in the fringe of the copse of trees which bordered the lane, covered by tarpaulins. Two policemen from the local *commissariat* were guarding the wreckage, which had been roped off, and Gautier went to speak to them.

'Do we know exactly what happened?'

'Not really, Inspector. Another party of diners from the restaurant were following not far behind the carriage. They heard the explosion, that's all.'

'They did not see the bomb being thrown? Nor anyone who might have thrown it?'

'No. It was a dark night.'

The bomb as a weapon of assassination was not new in Paris. In the 1890s, a wave of anarchy had swept through

Europe, and France, although it had not been engulfed by it, had not entirely escaped its effects. More than a dozen bombs had exploded in public places, including the Chamber of Deputies, a café near the Gare St Lazare, a police station and in several homes of judges and lawyers, ending with one which had killed the President of the Republic. On public occasions, the bombs were often thrown at their targets. At other times, they were left to explode by crude timing devices. In these latter cases, they often failed to explode, or did so at the wrong time, killing innocent people.

On balance, Gautier decided that the bomb which had killed de Périgord had probably not been thrown into the carriage by someone who had been waiting beside the lane for it to pass. Throwing a bomb into a passing carriage at night would be tricky. On the other hand, the assassin could easily have placed a bomb with a mechanical timing device in de Périgord's *calèche* earlier that evening, perhaps when he was at dinner. The coachman would have had to wait two hours or more for him and would probably have left the *calèche* outside the restaurant while he went off to drink with other coach drivers in a nearby bistro. Without any great expectations, Gautier looked among the wreckage of the *calèche* to see if he could find pieces of a bomb. Any fragments could be sent to the Government Scientific Laboratories, but in his experience, examinations made there seldom produced any results which would identify the person who had made a bomb.

He found nothing of any significance in the wreckage, so he asked the two policemen, 'Have either of you been here the whole night?'

'I have, Inspector. I was on night duty at the *commissariat* and they sent me here as soon as we heard about the bombing.'

'Then you saw the two bodies before they were taken away to the mortuary?'

'I did, yes.'

'How was the coachman dressed?'

'In livery. One could see that, even though the poor fellow was badly mutilated. He was dressed very correctly. See, there is the top-hat he was wearing.'

The policeman pointed towards the side of the lane, and Gautier saw the hat, which must have been blown away by the force of the exploding bomb and lay at the foot of a tree. A light tan in colour, it appeared almost undamaged.

Soon afterwards, Gautier left the Bois de Boulogne. The two policemen would remain by the wrecked carriage until officials from the laboratories which had been set up to deal with bombs during the wave of anarchy, arrived to inspect it. Removing the wreckage would be the responsibility of the local *commissariat*.

He did not drive directly to the Sûreté, but found a fiacre to take him to the Hôtel Meurice. Rodier, the head concierge, was on duty, and Gautier realized he had not heard of de Périgord's death. When he had been told, he took Gautier at once to the manager's office.

'Do you know yet who killed poor Yvette, Inspector?' the manager asked him.

'Not yet, but it seems certain that the snake must have been intended to kill Monsieur de Périgord.'

'What makes you think that?'

'Because de Périgord is dead.'

Briefly, Gautier told him about the bomb in the Bois de Boulogne. One could see in the manager's face as he listened that fearful fascination which news of sudden and violent death often arouses. He was a kind man, and learning that his hotel had lost a wealthy guest was not his first concern, although he may well have been relieved that de Périgord's death had not taken place on the premises.

'We need to inform Monsieur de Périgord's relatives,' Gautier said. 'Do you have his home address?'

'I do not believe so.'

'Does that mean that he stayed with you for the whole year?'

'No. He would leave Paris for the country every

summer for two or three months, but his suite was always kept for him and he left most of his clothes and many of his personal effects here.'

'Did he not give you a forwarding address for any mail that might arrive for him?'

'No. His instructions were that any letters and parcels should be kept here until he returned.'

'Very strange!'

'Monsieur de Périgord was a very private man, secretive, one might say. All I know is that he came from the town of Bergerac.'

'We may find something in his belongings which will tell us the names of his relations and where they can be reached.'

'I will take you up to his suite myself, Inspector.'

With the windows closed and the curtains still drawn, the air in de Périgord's suite was heavy and stale. Even after the manager had pulled the curtains back and opened a window, the atmosphere was oppressive and, it seemed to Gautier, unhealthy. He thought he could detect the smell of ether coming from the bathroom and mingling with it another odour which might have been incense or an exotic perfume. The covers of the bed had been turned down the previous evening and Gautier could imagine how fearful the chambermaid who had done it must have been, wondering whether she might find another snake there.

'Do you intend to search the whole suite?' the manager asked.

'Not now,' Gautier replied. He knew that a thorough search would have to be made, but that could be done later. 'All I am looking for now are letters or documents or an address book.'

He looked first of all in the bedroom, in the drawers of the dressing-table, the bedside table and the chest of drawers. Finding nothing there which would help him, he went to the writing table in the drawing-room where, on the night of Yvette's death, he had seen the press clipping about the French Ambassador in London. In one of the drawers, he found a supply of notepaper and envelopes, two sticks of sealing-wax and a heavy signet ring embossed with a coat of arms. As far as Gautier knew, de Périgord did not come of a family entitled to a coat of arms, but that need not have prevented him from adopting one. Many Frenchmen did, and the trappings of lineage would suit de Périgord's social pretensions.

In the other drawer, the clipping about the French Ambassador lay on top of a small stack of letters, invitations and visiting cards. Some of the invitations were printed on gilt-edged cards, others were *'petit bleus'*, sent through Paris's system of pneumatic tubes for express messages. The names of the hostesses who had sent the invitations were proof of de Périgord's standing in society, including as they did princesses, duchesses and countesses, as well as ladies from the leading bourgeois families. Gautier found himself wondering again how a bachelor from the provinces with no family connections nor any special literary or musical talents could have come to be accepted by the *gratin*. The only visiting card of any interest was that of the First Secretary of the American Embassy.

Among the letters, he saw an opened envelope addressed to de Périgord in a precise, carefully composed script. The letter inside the envelope was written in mauve ink on pink paper and carried an address in the town of Bergerac.

My dear Frédé,

As always, it was a delight to receive news of you, and I do appreciate your kindness in sparing the time from your busy social and literary life to write to your old, but always devoted aunt. As for me, my existence continues its pleasant but unexciting course. I am serving on a committee of ladies engaged in charitable work and at present we are busy raising funds for the relief of the misery caused by the recent epidemic of typhoid fever in North Africa.

One passage in your letter worried me. This was in the final paragraph in which you claim that your life is in danger. I find this hard to believe. The friends whose names you often mention in your letters come from the most highly respected families in France and nothing you have done could make people wish to harm you. If there is any fault in you, my dear boy, it is that you have always suffered from an excess of imagination and sensitivity. In any event, were your life really in danger, surely the Government would assist you. After all, you have done so much valuable work for them. Have you thought of asking the police for protection? My advice to you is to cast these morbid thoughts out of your mind.

I look forward to hearing from you again, and remain always your devoted and affectionate aunt,

Antoinette Lupin

When he had finished reading the letter, Gautier said to the manager, 'This should enable us to contact Monsieur de Périgord's relatives. I shall have to take it and all the other correspondence in the drawer away with me for closer examination.'

'By all means, Inspector. Let us take it down to my office and I will find a *portefeuille* in which you can carry it.'

The two men began emptying the drawer and bundling the invitations and letters together. The bottom of the drawer was lined with white paper, and as he lifted the last letter, Gautier felt a small, hard object which had been concealed beneath the lining. Pulling back the paper, he saw that it was a key.

He held it up and asked the manager, 'Have you any idea what this might be?'

'Yes, I recognize it. It is a key to one of the safety deposit boxes in our vaults.'

Gautier knew that, like many hotels, the Meurice had a strongroom fitted with small safes in which guests could deposit their valuables and money for safe-keeping. Each safe had two keys, one held by the guest and one by the management, and to ensure security, both keys would be required to open any one of them.

'We will need to open Monsieur de Périgord's safe,' he said.

The manager looked unhappy. 'I cannot allow that without the authority of my director. It is a strict rule of the hotel.'

'In that case, I will give you a letter from the Sûreté insisting that, since a case of murder is involved, the contents of the safety deposit be handed over to me.'

'Very well. That should suffice.'

They went to the manager's office and, while one of the assistant managers was sent to open de Périgord's safety deposit, Gautier composed and signed a letter authorizing the hotel to hand over whatever it contained. Presently, the assistant manager returned with a heavy, rectangular metal box. The box was locked, presumably as an additional precaution against theft, and Gautier supposed that de Périgord would have been carrying the key to it on his person at the time he was killed. He decided that he would take the box back to Sûreté headquarters, together with the briefcase which the manager had been filling with the correspondence they had found in the dead man's suite.

When he arrived back at his office, he found Surat waiting for him, and he could see that he had news to tell.

'I spoke once again to the waiter from the Hôtel Meurice last evening, as you asked me to, *patron*.'

'What did he have to say?'

'When I jogged his memory, he thought he remembered where he had seen the man with the plumber's tools before. He believes now that he was a coachman and that he had seen him more than once outside the hotel waiting to drive one of the guests staying there.'

'Did he say which guest?'

'Yes. The English banker, Sigmund Locke.'

'Locke had a coach, then, even though he does not live in Paris?'

'Yes, a Victoria. It is not actually his but belongs to the Paris branch of his bank.'

Gautier began writing a report on the murder of Armand de Périgord for the Director General. He had already arranged for a telegraph to be sent to the police in Bergerac, asking them to inform Madame Antoinette Lupin of her nephew's death and find out whether there were any other closer relatives who should also be notified and who would come to Paris to settle his affairs. The report he was preparing was longer than it need be. Experience had shown him that the fuller and more detailed a report was, the less likely Courtrand was to read it and to begin interfering in the investigation.

In one respect, he was fortunate, for Corbin had already told him that Courtrand would not be coming to his office that morning. He was to represent the Sûreté at a civic luncheon in honour of the Mayor of St Petersburg, who was on an official visit to Paris, and he needed the whole morning to prepare for the occasion. Gautier knew what that meant. Courtrand's servants would be cleaning and pressing his best morning coat and sash of office, while a barber would have been summoned to the house to trim his beard and wax his moustaches.

After finishing the report, Gautier spread de Périgord's invitations and letters, which he had brought back from the Hôtel Meurice, out on the top of his desk. The newspaper clipping about the French Ambassador's visit to Paris was among them, together with a later cutting of a report on the Ambassador's death. Pinned to the two clippings was a single sheet of notepaper on which had been written an unfinished letter, or perhaps a rough first draft of a letter, in what he recognized to be de Périgord's handwriting.

Madame,

I was shocked and desolated by the news of your husband's death and hasten to assure you of my

95

deepest sympathy. One can only hope that it was in no way connected with our friendship, for otherwise the burden of guilt would be insupportable. In these distressing circumstances, I realize that you will not wish to keep our rendezvous for next Tuesday, and indeed it might be prudent if we were to postpone seeing each other, at least

Just as Gautier had finished reading the draft letter, a civilian member of the Sûreté's staff came into the room. Jules was an engineer by vocation, who had developed an expert knowledge of locks and safes. So much so that people jokingly said he was employed by the Sûreté simply as a means of preventing him following a much more lucrative career in burglary. Gautier had sent for him so that he could open the metal box which had been found in de Périgord's safety deposit and brought back from the Hôtel Meurice. To have found the key to the box might have taken a long time, and Gautier could see no harm in using Jules's expertise to speed up his investigation.

Jules had brought with him a selection of tools and among them was a simple device which looked more like a piece of bent wire than a skeleton key. In less than a minute he had opened the box, and as he raised the lid, Gautier saw that it was full of money – bundles of banknotes and beneath them gold coins. One could tell at a glance that the total value of the hoard must run into many thousands of francs.

'What a place to keep cash!' Jules exclaimed scornfully. 'I could have opened this box with one of my wife's hatpins.'

'It was kept in a hotel's safety deposit.'

'Now what a spectacular robbery that would be! Breaking into a hotel's strongroom and emptying all the safety deposits! Not only money, but jewellery, bonds, share certificates. And it would be so simple to do! I've often thought about how it could be planned.'

Gautier laughed. 'Perhaps we should keep you on

permanent night duty here at headquarters, to prevent you being tempted to rob hotels.'

When Jules had left, Gautier emptied the contents of the cash box on to his desk. The bundled banknotes had been neatly arranged, and beneath the gold coins lay a large brown envelope. Inside the envelope was a sheaf of letters from the Bergerac branch of the Banque de France. Each letter acknowledged receipt of cash in varying amounts from Monsieur Armand de Périgord and confirmed that the money had been paid into his account at the bank.

Gautier saw that there was another letter in the brown envelope: a handwritten note addressed to de Périgord at the Hôtel Meurice and dated a few days previously, which must have been delivered by messenger. The paper on which the note had been written was faintly scented.

Chéri,

I have just heard that my husband is returning from Africa a week sooner that I had expected. Can we meet tomorrow afternoon instead of next Tuesday? Please say we can!

Léontine

After he had taken all the letters out of the brown envelope, Gautier could feel that there was still something inside it. When he held it upside down and shook it, two photographs slipped out and fell face down on to his desk. Even before he turned them over, he guessed that one must be a photograph of Catriona Becker. He was right, and the other was of the Comtesse de Chartres, posing in the nude.

Chapter 10

The café in Place Dauphine was almost empty at lunch-
time that day. Often, and particularly when there was a
major criminal trial in the nearby Palais de Justice, it
could be uncomfortably crowded and noisy, with customers calling for food or wine and talking excitedly
about what they had seen in court. Gautier could not
recall when he had first begun eating in the café. At that
time it had been owned by a woman from Normandy and
her daughter Janine. The cuisine had been excellent,
and after Suzanne had left him, he and Janine had become
lovers, but then she had returned to Normandy and, so
people said, married a farmer. Now only force of habit
drew Gautier to the café, for all it had to offer was
the reassurance of familiarity, nostalgic memories and
a pleasant view of the chestnut trees which bordered
Place Dauphine.

He had brought the two photographs which he had
found in de Périgord's cash box with him, and as he was
eating he studied the one of Catriona Becker. When she
had told him of the photograph, Catriona had implied
that it was innocent enough and that it was only the
suggestive décor of the room in which she had posed
which would have shocked her American fiancé had he
seen it. Gautier could see now that she had been telling
only part of the truth. On the wall of the room behind
her in the photograph hung an oil painting of a naked
woman, but neither it nor anything else in the background
would be described as erotic. Catriona had said she had
not posed in the nude. That was also true, but she had

been dressed in the costume of a nymph, wearing only a short diaphanous tunic and with artificial flowers entwined in her hair. One could well imagine a man from the Bible belt of America being horrified by the sight of her bare arms and legs and by her pose, reclining on a sofa. To Gautier, though, it only looked ridiculous.

The photograph of the Comtesse de Chartres showed that she had been rash enough to allow herself to be photographed naked. In posing, she seemed to be imitating the nude in the oil painting hanging behind her. No doubt the pose had been intended to be lascivious and seductive, but it looked merely vulgar. Gautier was not really sure why. It may have been that her beauty had been cheapened by the vague and fatuous expression on her face. He wondered whether she had been drinking or was drugged.

He was becoming intrigued by the life de Périgord had led. In spite of rumours that he was homosexual, he had been involved with at least three women – Catriona Becker, the Comtesse de Chartres and Madame Deslandes – and very probably two others, the wife of Sigmund Locke and Madame Léontine Colbert. Gautier was well aware that women might not necessarily be repelled by effeminacy, but clearly de Périgord must have possessed other qualities which attracted them. Whatever they were, he had used them skilfully, trapping women in a web of infidelity and deceit which made them hopelessly vulnerable to exploitation.

In spite of what Catriona Becker had said, it appeared inconceivable now that de Périgord had not been in some way involved in blackmailing both her and the Comtesse. Why else would he have kept the photograph he had taken of her locked securely in his safety deposit? And why else should he have lied to her about it? The substantial sum in banknotes also needed explaining. Even if he had not sent the demands for money himself, he must at the very least have been in league with the blackmailer.

When he arrived back in his office, he telephoned Catriona Becker. The telephone operator was in a poor humour and he had to be patient as she took several minutes to connect him. In a service that was still relatively new, the telephonists, believing that they were indispensable, had invested themselves with a power that was rapidly becoming intolerable. They worked grudgingly, and if they felt they were not being given a proper respect, would delay a call indefinitely. When finally Gautier was connected to Catriona Becker's telephone, he had another struggle to make himself understood by her Scottish maid.

Catriona's voice, when at last he heard it, was bright and cheerful. 'I know why you are telephoning. We forgot to arrange a time for your next English lesson.'

'We did,' Gautier replied, 'but that is not the reason for my call. I regret that I have bad news for you.'

'What news?'

'Your friend, Monsieur de Périgord, is dead. He was killed by a bomb late last night.'

'God in heaven!'

Catriona listened as Gautier told her how de Périgord had been murdered. From time to time, she asked a question, as though she wished to form a detailed picture of the bombing, the exact place in the Bois de Boulogne where it had occurred, whether de Périgord had died immediately, who else had been killed. Gautier had the feeling that she was not as surprised or shocked as one might have expected, but he dismissed the thought as no more than a policeman's habitual suspicion.

Finally she asked him, 'Do you know what time this happened?'

'It must have been shortly before eleven.'

'Eleven? Are you certain?'

'As near as we can tell.'

'That means that you were here with me in my apartment when the bomb was thrown.'

'It would appear so.' As he was speaking, he remembered her insistence that he should stay and dine with her after the English lesson. He added, 'In view of what has happened, I shall need to talk to you again about the matter we discussed last night.'

100

'What matter?'

'I am sure you remember.' One could not be certain that the telephone operator was not listening to their conversation. 'It concerns you and the Comtesse de Chartres.'

'Why do you wish to talk about that now?'

'What you told me may well have a bearing on Monsieur de Périgord's death. If it were convenient, I could come round to your apartment now.'

'No,' Catriona said at once, 'that would not be possible, I am afraid. I am expecting friends to call on me at any minute.'

'Then later?'

'I'm sorry. I have an engagement for dinner. And for that reason we will not be able to have an English lesson today.'

'I will see you tomorrow then, but no later, please. This is a murder investigation.'

'Very well, if you really believe I can help you.'

Gautier realized that he could have insisted on speaking to Catriona that afternoon or evening, but if he had, she might have taken offence and been less willing to answer his questions frankly. One also had to remember that she was a friend of the Prefect of Police. When he had first joined the Sûreté, he had felt that, as a matter of principle, the department should not give important people any special treatment. As he had been promoted to senior posts, he had begun to realize that diplomacy was sometimes more efficacious than principles in achieving one's ends. In this instance, a day's delay would not be serious as he had other investigations to make which were likely to prove more fruitful.

Not until several minutes later did he realize that the next day would be a Sunday. Catriona would know that he would not call at her home on a Sunday. His interest in her problems of blackmail was not an official police matter, and were he to intrude in her private life on a Sunday, she would have a reason for complaining to the Prefect. He wondered whether she had not pointed out that the next day was Sunday deliberately, in order to give herself a reprieve of twenty-four hours before she must answer more questions.

Whatever the truth, he decided he did not have to wait idly until he saw her on Monday. There must be other ways of learning more about de Périgord's life and activities, and one of these might be to visit his *garçonnière*. So, leaving the Sûreté and the Ile de la Cité, he boarded a horse-drawn omnibus which would take him in the direction of Rue des Moines.

Climbing the stairs to the *impériale* or upper deck while the omnibus was travelling at speed needed sureness of foot and balance, and Gautier found himself realizing that he was not as young or as agile as he once had been. Despite this discomfort, however, Gautier was fond of this method of transport. The disappearance of the horse from Paris, which could not be far ahead, would rob the city of some of its character. People said they could look forward to cleaner streets when horses were no longer there to foul them, but the internal combustion engine with its fumes might bring pollution that was even more harmful.

The apartment which de Périgord used for his amorous pastimes was in an old building which had escaped destruction fifty years previously when Baron Haussmann, on the instructions of Napoléon III, had razed a large part of Paris to make a new city of broad boulevards and avenues and triumphal arches. The concierge met Gautier with the customary laconic suspicion, but admitted that an apartment on the second floor of the building was rented to a Monsieur Armand de Périgord. She was a little sparrow of a woman, with a beak of a nose and busy inquisitive eyes. Her husband, one suspected, would not be allowed to spend many peaceful, undisturbed evenings. When Gautier told her that de Périgord was dead and explained how he had died, she only shrugged her shoulders.

'You do not seem to be surprised, Madame,' Gautier remarked.

102

'Eventually some *cocu* was bound to take his revenge.'

'*Cocu*?'

'The ladies my tenant entertained were all of an age to be married.'

'Were there many of them?'

'Plenty.' The concierge made a small noise of disapproval. 'He must have had some hidden talents, that one.'

She agreed to take Gautier up to the second floor of the building and let him into the apartment. For a *garçonnière*, it was larger than one might have expected, with a spacious drawing-room, a dining-room, two bedrooms and a kitchen, all neatly but not extravagantly furnished. The only encouragements to lasciviousness were the painting of a nude, which Gautier had already seen in the photograph of Catriona, and in one of the bedrooms an immense bed with silk sheets, strewn with brightly coloured cushions. In general, the décor was not one which Gautier would have thought might appeal to ladies of taste and discernment, but then he supposed that any ladies who thought they were in love might well suspend their judgement as well as their virtue.

The concierge had been watching Gautier as he made his brief inspection, and now he asked her, 'At what time did your tenant entertain these ladies?'

'Always in the late afternoon.'

'And how did they come here?'

'In his carriage. One supposes that he must have sent his coachman to collect them from their homes and bring them here. They would slip out of the carriage and past my lodge quickly, as though they were afraid of being seen. But if he has been murdered, it must surely mean that someone must have found out.'

'The coachman who drove them here would have known of their visits.'

'Of course, but Monsieur de Périgord could surely have relied on him. After all, he was his servant.'

'His servant?'

'Yes. Lucien. He lives here in the apartment, cleans the

place and sometimes cooks as well. Monsieur de Périgord brought him here from Bergerac. An insolent creature Lucien is, I can tell you. Has grand ideas, dresses and behaves like a gentleman when he's not working. He and I have quarrelled more than once, I can tell you.'

'Well, Madame, I regret to tell you that you will not quarrel with him again. He also was killed by the bomb.'

'Lucien?' The concierge looked at Gautier incredulously. 'He's not dead! He spent the night here as usual. Why, I saw him leaving the building only an hour or two ago.'

'Are we talking about the same man?'

'Lucien? Of course. There is no other.'

'And you say he drives Monsieur de Périgord's carriage?'

'All I can tell you is that he was always driving it every time a lady came in the coach to the apartment.'

Gautier said nothing for a time, trying to work out the implications of what he had heard. His silence must have been interpreted by the concierge as doubt, for she said, 'If you do not believe me, Monsieur, I will prove it. Come with me.'

They had been talking in the drawing-room of the apartment and now she led him into the smaller of the two bedrooms and opened a wardrobe which stood against one wall. Hanging inside it were a brown coachman's coat and breeches and on a shelf above them a brown top-hat and a whip.

'When do you suppose this Lucien will be returning to the apartment?' Gautier asked.

'Late tonight, I dare say. Monsieur de Périgord always allows him to have Saturday afternoon free. He usually dresses up in his best clothes and goes out; drinking, no doubt, or to a café concert or music-hall. Sometimes he even has the impudence to bring a girl back here with him for the night; smuggles them in and thinks I haven't seen him.'

'Why the secrecy? Monsieur de Périgord never spent the night here, did he?'

104

'Never. But he would scarcely be pleased if he knew Lucien was bringing whores to the apartment. Mind you, sometimes he treated Lucien more like a brother than a servant.' She stared defiantly at Gautier, and her next remark was heavy with innuendo. 'Perhaps they were even closer than brothers.'

The concierge was clearly in a mood to gossip. Learning that de Périgord was dead seemed to have freed her of the constraints which might have prevented her talking about one of her tenants. Now she was eager to grumble, to complain and to astonish. Gautier listened, discounting much of what she told him, but even so, trying to form a picture of the life of de Périgord and his servant.

When he had heard enough, he left Rue des Moines and returned to the Sûreté, where he found Surat waiting for him. The search of de Périgord's suite at the Hôtel Meurice had produced nothing further which might have been connected with his murder, and his belongings were now being stored by the hotel's staff until his relatives could collect them. The suite would then be cleaned and made available for occupation by other guests.

After supervising the search, Surat had, on his own initiative, gone to the offices of the Compagnie Générale des Fiacres, from which de Périgord had been hiring his carriage, for it had occurred to him that the company may not have been informed of the destruction of one of their vehicles and the death of the coachman. He had also begun to wonder, once he had heard that the driver of the *calèche* had been wearing brown livery, whether the dead man might have been Laborde; the Laborde who bought the cobra and smuggled it into the Hôtel Meurice and whose visiting cards had been ordered from the printer Buisson.

'Did you know,' he said to Gautier, 'that the company owns more than two-thirds of all the fiacres in Paris? Why, they employ more than one hundred and fifty people in their offices and one hundred and fifty inspectors!'

Gautier had to listen while Surat unburdened his amazement at the scale of the Compagnie Générale's operations. Almost 1,000 men, he said, worked in the coach-building yard, while 200 blacksmiths were required to shoe the horses and 900 grooms to look after them.

'Their stables are so magnificent that English tourists are taken to admire them.'

'And Laborde?' Gautier asked patiently when the exposé was over.

'The driver of the coach which was destroyed by the bomb could not have been the man for whom we are looking. Poor fellow, he was short, with a pot belly and inclined to drink too freely.'

'Was he the only one who ever drove de Périgord?'

'From the company, yes. But because he used the *calèche* so frequently, de Périgord would often have his own servant drive. He was not willing to pay for two coachmen from the company.'

'Or so he said.'

'I found out one more thing. De Périgord provided a suit of livery for the company's coachman to wear – light brown livery.'

'As well as for his servant.'

Gautier told Surat of his visit to the apartment in Rue des Moines and what he had learnt about de Périgord's servant, Lucien. 'Arrange for an officer to go round to the apartment first thing tomorrow morning,' he added, 'and bring the man in for questioning.'

'Tomorrow is Sunday, *patron*.'

'I know, but we must speak to this Lucien as soon as we can.'

'I'll bring him in myself.'

'That won't be necessary. In any case, I have another and more important task for you.'

Among the records kept at Sûreté headquarters were files on all people convicted of criminal offences involving explosives. Gautier told Surat to arrange for a check to be made on all such offenders who had been freed from prison, as well as on all persons suspected of having made or supplied explosives during the campaigns of the anarchists. The number of people in Paris with the knowledge and skill to make an effective bomb must be limited.

After Surat had left his office, a messenger came in bringing a telegraph message which had just arrived from the police in Bergerac. The message read:

MADAME ANTOINETTE LUPIN HAS BEEN INFORMED OF THE DEATH OF HER NEPHEW, ARMAND DE PÉRIGORD. SHE IS HIS ONLY SURVIVING RELATIVE IN BERGERAC AS BOTH HIS PARENTS DIED SOME YEARS AGO. MADAME LUPIN HAS AGREED TO COME TO PARIS TO MAKE ARRANGEMENTS FOR HIS INTERMENT AND TO SETTLE HIS AFFAIRS. SHE WILL BE TRAVELLING BY TRAIN ON MONDAY AND WILL CONTACT THE SÛRETÉ ON ARRIVAL.

Chapter 11

Sunday had always been for Gautier a day to be enjoyed for the small luxuries it offered. In the early days of their marriage, Suzanne and he would join her parents, her sister and her sister's husband for Mass, and afterwards old Monsieur Dubois would take them all out to lunch in some good bourgeois restaurant, a lunch which always ended with the luxury of an excellent cigar and a glass of fine old Armagnac. Those days were over, but there were still small luxuries he could enjoy on his own. One was lying in bed a few minutes longer, savouring the silence in the streets outside his apartment. Another was the luxury of having himself shaved. He had discovered an enterprising barber who opened his shop on Sundays, mainly for travellers arriving at the nearby Gare St Lazare, and he had become a regular customer.

This Sunday, as he sat in the barber's chair, he was thinking not of the past but of the changing complications in the de Périgord affair. He had begun by investigating a crime, the killing, perhaps unintentional, of the hotel maid Yvette. Then, at the instigation of the Prefect of Police, he had gone to the aid of a lady who was being blackmailed. Now both investigations had been fused together and he was confronted by a more serious crime, one which would attract enough public attention to demand an urgent solution.

De Périgord's servant Lucien might be the person best placed to point out the direction Gautier's investigation should take. He had driven the ladies to their clandestine meetings with de Périgord in the *garçonnière*, and one could not discount the possibility that the two men had engineered the blackmail plot together. He would be brought to Sûreté headquarters next morning, but if he was as insolent as the concierge had suggested, he might well defy attempts to prise information out of him. Gautier would be in a stronger position when questioning him the following morning if he knew more about the mechanics of the plot: how the ladies had been collected and conveyed to Rue des Moines, how they had been smuggled back to the centre of Paris afterwards and whether they knew that the man driving them was de Périgord's servant.

Logically, he should speak again to Catriona Becker before he interviewed Lucien, and his irritation with her for the way she had put off seeing him returned. Then, as he left the barber's shop, the sight of the church of St Augustin stretching up into the sky in front of him gave him an idea. He recalled that some time ago when he was in that *quartier*, noticing a Presbyterian church in a small street just north of Boulevard de Courcelles. He also recalled Catriona Becker, when she was talking of the American she planned to marry, telling him that she was a Presbyterian. Since she lived not far from Boulevard de Courcelles, he wondered whether she might not use the church for her religious devotions and whether she might be there that Sunday morning. It was no more than a slender possibility, but even so, as he had nothing more urgent to do, worth exploring.

The church was a simple, drab brick building and when he reached it Gautier could tell from the carriages waiting in the street outside that the Sunday's divine service – he knew the Scots did not talk of Mass – must still be in progress. The number of carriages surprised him, for he had not thought that there were many Scots living in Paris. The only one who had made any impression on him, apart from Catriona, was a kilted Highlander who could be seen standing outside the Irish-American bar playing his bagpipes to attract customers. The bar, which had been opened not long previously, was intended

109

largely to cater for visiting Americans and almost the only Frenchmen who patronized it were from the horse-racing fraternity.

He had to wait for more than half an hour before the service ended and the congregation began to leave the church. As they did, Gautier saw that his speculative journey had not been in vain, for Catriona Becker was one of the first women to emerge. Once in the street, she paused for a moment to see where her carriage was stationed and then began walking towards it. When Gautier intercepted her, she stared at him.

'Jean-Paul! What are you doing here?'

Gautier was not aware that she even knew his Christian name, but her using it suggested at least that she was not displeased to find him there. He said, 'I came to meet you, Madame. Did you not agree that I might speak to you today?'

Catriona laughed. 'You are persistent, are you not? Do you often work on Sundays?'

'Frequently. Sadly, criminals seldom observe the Sabbath.'

'What does your wife think about it?'

'My wife died some years ago.'

'I'm so sorry.' She reached out and touched his arm. 'Now how can I help you?'

Knowing that he had been receiving her pity on false pretences gave Gautier no more than a fleeting pang of guilt. Had she known the circumstances which had led to Suzanne's death, she might still have pitied him. 'The questions I wish to ask you need not take long.'

'In that case, you may as well ask them in my carriage on my way home,' Catriona said. Then she changed her mind. 'No, I have a better idea. It is such a lovely morning, let us take a walk in Parc Monceau. I need the exercise and I dare say you do, since you have no wife to look after your health.'

When they reached her carriage she told the coachman that she would not be needing him and they set out to walk the short distance to Parc Monceau. Gautier found himself wishing she had not chosen the park for their walk. Claire Ryan's father, the Earl of Newry, lived in a ground-floor apartment which backed on to Parc Monceau and it was there that he had first met Claire. He had no wish to be reminded that Claire had left Paris and that the chances of their ever meeting again were remote. He wondered too what the Earl would think were he to look out from a window and see him strolling in the park with another young and attractive woman.

As they walked towards it, Catriona chatted light-heartedly. She described an incident during the church service when the elderly and short-sighted minister had dropped the Bible from which he was reading, reopened it at a different and wholly inappropriate book of one of the prophets and continued reading without noticing his mistake. She seemed to find the incident far more amusing than Gautier would have done, but he supposed that amusement would be scarce in a Presbyterian church.

When they were strolling round the perimeter of the park, she said mockingly, 'Now, Inspector, you may begin your cross-examination.'

'Hardly a cross-examination, Madame. I just need a few facts.'

'You do not suspect me then of having murdered poor Armand?'

'My questions are not concerned with his death, at least not directly. You see, we are certain now that it was de Périgord who was blackmailing you.'

'How do you know that?'

'We found a very large sum of money in his safety deposit at the hotel where he was living, as well as evidence that he had been making substantial regular deposits to a bank outside of Paris.'

'Might that not be money he had earned?'

'By writing poetry and interpreting? I would scarcely think so. We also found this photograph.'

Gautier had brought with him the photograph of Catriona which de Périgord had taken in his *garçonnière*. When he showed it to her she stared at it incredulously

111

for a moment. Then her expression hardened.

'This is the photograph which Armand said had been stolen. So he had it all the time.'

'Did you never suspect that he was the blackmailer?'

'I did, but I persuaded myself that it could not possibly have been him. He was always so kind and considerate to me that I had to give him the benefit of the doubt.' She paused and looked at Gautier as though wondering how her next remark would be received. 'And now he is dead. My nightmare is over.'

'You would be unwise to rely on that. We believe that his servant may have been implicated in the extortion.'

'What servant?' Catriona asked sharply.

'His coachman. A man named Lucien. I would not be at all surprised if Lucien was involved in blackmailing you and the Comtesse de Chartres, or at the very least that he was aware of it. I want you to tell me everything about your visit to de Périgord's apartment. How did you travel there?'

De Périgord had worked out a plan, Catriona told him, by which she could make her visit to his apartment in secret. After the lunch party at which they were both guests, she had taken a fiacre to the shop of a well-known jeweller near Place Vendôme. There she had spent a full half-hour being shown some of the jeweller's latest pieces, rings, necklaces and tiaras. When finally she left the shop, de Périgord's *calèche* was waiting in the street outside and she was driven in it to Rue des Moines. At the end of the afternoon, she was driven into the centre of Paris and dropped off by the Café de la Paix, where she knew she would find a fiacre to take her home.

'As I have already told you, my visit to his apartment was just an adventure, and the secrecy made it more exciting.'

'Do you know whether a similar arrangement was made for the visits of the Comtesse de Chartres?'

'Yes, very similar. Maria told me so.'

'And how did you pay the blackmail money which was demanded? What instructions were you given?'

'They were very precise and I followed them exactly. I was to make a parcel of the fifty thousand francs, all in banknotes, and leave the parcel in the Bois de Boulogne.'

Catriona had been told that on a day named in the blackmail note, a Monday, she must go unaccompanied to the Bois de Boulogne, and that she must be driven there not in her carriage, but in a fiacre. Once in the Bois, she must leave the parcel of money at the foot of a tree in a small copse. Both the copse and the tree were shown in a rough sketch attached to the blackmail demand. After placing the parcel by the tree, she must leave the Bois at once, in the same fiacre which had taken her there. Should she attempt to wait and watch for the parcel to be collected, the photograph of her and an account of her afternoon with de Périgord would be sent to her fiancé in America.

'And you followed these instructions?' Gautier asked her.

'Yes and no. I did not wait to see who collected the parcel, but I arranged for someone else to do so.'

'Who was that?'

'My coachman François. He is a wonderful old man, loyal and absolutely trustworthy. I went to the Bois in a fiacre, but François took the coach and drove through it, passing the copse where I was to leave the money slowly, so that he could see who collected it.' Catriona smiled as she added, 'My maid dressed up in her best clothes and went with him as a passenger, for an empty coach might have seemed suspicious.'

'And they saw someone pick up the parcel?'

'Yes. You won't believe this, but it was a little urchin. François saw him pick it up and run off.'

'He had been paid to collect the parcel, no doubt, and take it to someone who was waiting some distance away.'

'Possibly. Or he may have taken it straight to the hotel.'

'The hotel?'

'Yes. The instructions which came with the black-mailer's demand said that the parcel was to be addressed to a hotel.'

'Which hotel?'

Catriona shrugged. 'I really cannot remember. It was a very commonplace name; of a poet or playwright, I believe. The Hôtel Voltaire or Racine or some name like that.'

'Did you not also have to put on the parcel the name of the person for whom it was intended?'

'No. Just the name of the hotel and beneath it three crosses in red ink. Strange, was it not?'

The fact that she could not remember the name of the hotel irritated Gautier but did not surprise him. He had already come to accept the inconstancy of Catriona's moods, alternating as they did between thoughtfulness and a whimsical insouciance. She had gone to some trouble to discover who would collect the parcel of money she left in the Bois de Boulogne, but could not recall what might have been vital in helping to identify the blackmailer. At the same time, as a policeman Gautier knew he should not discount the possibility that she might be deliberately withholding that information.

During the remainder of their walk through Parc Monceau, she chatted cheerfully. She appeared satisfied now that the threat of blackmail had vanished and she could resume her carefree social life. Gautier had read in the newspapers that an American circus troupe was soon to give a short season in Paris, and Catriona told him that she was to be one of the patrons of a special gala performance for charity.

'What does the patronage entail?' Gautier asked her.

'Financing the performance. The circus people give their services free and the patrons cover all the other costs so that all the takings can be given to charity. The gala will be a major event in the social calendar. All Paris will be there.'

'Where is it to be held?'

'In the Cirque Alfredi.' Catriona may have felt that Gautier was not as impressed as he should have been by what she had told him, for she added, 'To be invited to be a patron is a great honour. They only asked me because I am marrying an American.'

114

'The fact that you can afford the honour may be another reason.'

Catriona laughed. 'Such a cynical remark is not worthy of you, Jean-Paul. Take care or I shall not ask you to join me and my friends in my patron's box at the gala.'

As they left the park and headed for her apartment, Gautier found himself envying her her good spirits, her infectious laugh, her walk, the jaunty angle at which she held her parasol. It was as though she had, as she herself had said, escaped from a bad dream. And yet he had a feeling, not strong enough to be called a premonition, that perhaps her relief might be premature.

As they approached her apartment, he noticed her glancing at him sideways, and then she said, 'There is no reason why we should not continue with your English lessons.'

'I cannot possibly impose on you any further,' Gautier replied. They both knew that her offering to give him the lessons had only been a device contrived by the Prefect of Police, in the hope that Gautier would be able to extricate her from the blackmailer's grasp.

'It is no imposition, I enjoy them. Come and see me in a day or so and you can tell me how your investigation into the death of poor Armand is progressing.'

When he reached Sûreté headquarters, the two officers who had been sent to bring de Périgord's servant in for questioning were waiting for him. He could tell at once that something had gone wrong.

'The man Lucien has left the apartment in Rue des Moines,' one of the men told him.

'He was not there?'

'No. The concierge says he returned to the apartment yesterday evening earlier than she had expected, hurriedly packed his belongings in a valise and left. He did not tell her where he was going.'

Chapter 12

'I am still amazed by that man!' Surat told Gautier. 'He was proud and arrogant and most people believed he was a *pédé*. Yet he seems to have been able to seduce any woman almost at will.'

'We poor men,' Gautier replied, 'can never hope to divine the workings of a woman's mind. Women can become besotted, abandon all taste and discrimination, over a man who most of us would find unsympathetic.'

'Look at that girl who just passed us. Not a great beauty perhaps, but watch the way she walks, the swing of her hips. She may well be no more than a shop assistant, from La Samaritaine perhaps, but what style! What powers of seduction!'

'You had better not allow your wife to hear you talking like that,' Gautier teased him.

'Why not? Twenty years ago my wife might have been that girl. And to think that even she might be a willing victim for a man as distasteful as de Périgord.'

'Old friend,' Gautier replied, 'you should have learnt by now that women are guided not by logic but by their instincts.'

The two of them were standing on Pont St Michel and gazing down at the Seine as they talked. They had met on the bridge by chance, for Surat had been returning to the Sûreté after buying a book which his daughter needed from an educational bookshop on the Left Bank. His daughter, an exceptionally clever girl, was studying mathematics at the Sorbonne. When Surat had explained guiltily where he had been, Gautier reminded him of the many

116

occasions when he had worked long into the night. Then he had added, with a smile, that he himself was on his way to the Café Corneille.

'There is something you can do as soon as you are back at headquarters,' he went on to say. 'De Périgord's servant has disappeared and we must find him. Arrange for the police in all the *arrondissements* to be alerted. Go to see de Périgord's concierge, who will be able to give you a description of the man. While you are there, search the apartment as well, for you may find something which will give us a clue as to where he has bolted.'

'Might he not have left Paris?'

'Possibly. On the other hand, he has almost certainly been helping de Périgord to blackmail some of his lady friends and he may be hoping to squeeze a little more cash out of them before he leaves the city.'

'Who are these unfortunate ladies?'

'I only know of two: the Comtesse de Chartres and Madame Catriona Becker. But I suspect that Madame Colbert may have been intended as another.'

Gautier told Surat of the note from Madame Colbert which de Périgord had kept locked in his safety deposit, together with the photographs of Comtesse Maria and Catriona Becker. Although he could only speculate on its significance, he also gave him a summary of the draft letter which de Périgord had been composing to Madame Deslandes.

'It sounds as though he was intending to end his affair with the Ambassador's widow,' Surat remarked.

'Yes. The woman appears to have completely lost her head over him, but once she had decided to leave her husband for him, she would not be vulnerable to blackmail. Her husband's suicide gave de Périgord an excuse for breaking off from her.'

'The man was a monster! Cunning and treacherous!'

'Well, his treachery seems to have caught up with him.'

'And we are left with the task of bringing whoever killed him to justice.'

After they had parted and Gautier was on his way

117

to Boulevard St Germain, he thought about Surat's last comment. Enforcing the law and bringing wrongdoers to justice was an essential function in any civilized society and one which, he liked to believe, he performed competently. That was not to say that it always brought satisfaction. There were crimes which he could understand, even if he could not condone: a knife thrust by a woman driven out of control by cruelty or humiliation; theft by a man to relieve the misery that poverty was bringing on his family; even the bomb of the agitator who believed it would right the wrongs of society.

Not infrequently, he could feel sympathy for the criminals in such cases, even though he accepted that they must be punished. But now he had to direct his energy and skill to the investigation of crimes which centred on the frailties of people who indulged themselves in adultery and intrigue and petty vice. Only a day or two previously, at the instigation of the Prefect of Police, he had been trying to help a woman who was being blackmailed. Now he had to investigate the murder of the blackmailer. If there was a kind of irony in this, it was one which Gautier did not appreciate.

When he reached the Café Corneille, he saw that Duthrey was sitting alone at a table reading a copy of a rival newspaper. Although he was an older man, Duthrey was the closest of the friends he met at the café. From time to time, they would dine or go to the theatre together, and more than once he had been allowed to search through *Figaro*'s library of back numbers, looking for information he could not obtain elsewhere. Today, as usual, they shook hands and then went through the Frenchman's routine of exchanging enquiries and complaints about their livers.

As Gautier was ordering an aperitif, Duthrey asked him, 'Did I gather the other day that you were intending to speak to Sigmund Locke?'

'Yes, I saw him at the Ritz soon after you had.'

'May I ask why? I have no wish to breach confidentiality, of course.'

118

'It was a routine enquiry. One of the staff at the Hôtel Meurice had been killed during the previous night and I wondered whether he or Madame Locke had seen or heard anything,' Gautier replied. Then he added, 'And you, what is your interest in Monsieur Locke?'

Duthrey gave a small snort of contempt. 'I have no interest in him. As I told you, my colleague on *Figaro* had arranged to interview him but could not go. It's a trifling matter.'

'To do with finance, I assume?'

'Ostensibly so, but more to do with politics.'

He told Gautier that *Figaro* was curious to know why Locke had visited Paris so often in the past few weeks. He was known to have had meetings at a very high level with more than one Government ministry.

'My colleague is an anglophobe. He suspects that France may have made a secret financial deal with the English as part of the Entente Cordiale and that Locke's bank may have some role in it.'

'Our national suspicion of the English is becoming an obsession.'

'Be careful!' Duthrey teased him. 'Or we will begin to wonder which side you are on. Is it the love of their language which has suborned you into this treachery, or of their women? The gossip column in our paper tells me you recently escorted a Scottish lady to the soirée of Princesse Hélène.'

Gautier decided to ignore the quip. 'Since we are talking of British women, what do you know of Madame Locke?'

'She is beautiful and very much younger than he. People believe it was she who won him invitations to royal country-house parties in England.'

'Are you saying she is a friend of Edward?'

'One of many.' Duthrey chuckled. 'In London society, they say that any woman who has not slept with Edward is a laughing-stock.'

While they were talking, another of their friends arrived at the café. Froissart, the bookseller, was accompanied by

119

a cousin of his named Fénélon, who also had a bookshop but in Caen. Fénélon was on his first visit to Paris, and his provincial's distrust of the capital was slowly succumbing to admiration for the sights and spectacles he was seeing. Thinking perhaps that those who lived in Paris might not be aware of them, he described in detail how it felt to be looking down on the city from the top of the Eiffel Tower, the richness of the art treasures in the Louvre and the extraordinary deftness with which animals were despatched in the abattoirs.

'Ours is truly a remarkable city,' Duthrey agreed politely.

Fénélon, afraid perhaps that he was being too lavish with his admiration, said, 'But dangerous.'

'Dangerous? How so?'

'We may live in the provinces, but we are well informed. Everyone in Caen knows of the political unrest in Paris, of the anarchists and their bombs.'

'All that is over,' Duthrey told him. 'For the past ten years anarchists have been no threat.'

'Then who was responsible for that bomb in the Bois de Boulogne the other evening? The newspapers say that the man killed was a poet. We all know that poets and writers are often associated with anarchist movements.'

'Armand de Périgord was no anarchist. He lived permanently in one of Paris's most expensive hotels and moved in the most exclusive social circles.'

'I once published a book of his,' Froissart remarked. He may have been trying to divert the conversation away from the bomb, thinking that it might be placing Gautier in a difficult position.

'What kind of book was it?' Gautier asked.

'A volume of verse; not original poems but translations of poetry written in other languages: mainly Greek, Latin and English.'

'Were the poems which he translated homosexual in theme?'

'Many of them and others were the work of poets who were known to have been homosexual. That may be why everyone concluded that de Périgord must be a *pédé* himself.'

'Did the book sell well?' Gautier asked.

'He certainly could not have lived on his literary earnings,' Froissart replied. 'Occasionally, some of his work would be published in literary reviews, but there is no money in that.'

'Perhaps when Gautier has mastered the English language, he might try his hand at translating Irish poetry.'

'It is all I can do,' Gautier replied, 'to struggle through the *New York Herald*.'

'I've taken to reading that absurd paper from time to time,' Froissart said. 'The other day, it informed me that John D. Rockefeller has a greater annual income than all the crowned heads of Europe put together.'

Duthrey snorted. 'Not content with parading their wealth, the Americans are aiming to debase our traditional institutions. We are to be exposed to an American circus!'

'What circus?'

'It is not a circus in the true sense,' Froissart said. 'They call it a Wild West Show. Cowboys demonstrate their skills with horses and lassos and stage mock battles with Red Indians.'

'Americans can never match the French circus with its athleticism, skill, daring and grace, let alone the beauty of our lady riders.'

Gautier listened as his friends began to reminisce about great French circus performers of the past. He was glad that everyone appeared to have forgotten about Armand de Périgord. No one even seemed to find it odd that a man whom they had been discussing at the café only a few days previously should have been murdered and in such a dramatic fashion.

As often happened, he and Duthrey left the café together, and while they were walking along Boulevard St Germain, Duthrey remarked, 'I was surprised when you told me that Locke had been staying at the Hôtel Meurice. I would have thought that the Ritz is much more

121

his style of hotel. Like the hotel, he has an aura of immense dignity and wealth.'

'I understand he usually stays at the Ritz, but had decided to try the Meurice on this occasion.'

'He is a difficult man for a journalist to interview; a banker who keeps his mouth shut as tightly as his purse. On the other hand, I found him most courteous and considerate. Do you know that after our interview he insisted on having me driven back to our office in his carriage?'

'I am told he always has a carriage at his disposal.'

'Yes, it was waiting outside the hotel in Place Vendôme; a magnificent Victoria with a negro coachman.'

'A negro?'

'Yes, from Senegal. Apparently, the man used to work as a messenger in the Dakar branch of Locke's bank, but married a French girl, so the company found him employment in Paris.'

Before going to lunch, Gautier called in at the Sûreté in case there might be any messages, and was told that a Madame Antoinette Lupin was waiting to see him. He recognized her at once as the elderly lady in a toque hat whose photograph he had seen in de Périgord's suite at the Hôtel Meurice. She was wearing a toque hat again now, this time a black one.

After introducing himself, Gautier said, 'I must apologize, Madame, for not being in my office when you arrived.'

'That was my fault, not yours.' Although she looked frail, Madame Lupin's handshake and her voice were firm and steady. 'I had not expected to be in Paris until the afternoon, but I caught an earlier train.'

'This is a sad occasion for you, Madame. You have my department's deepest sympathy.' Madame Lupin nodded to acknowledge the courtesy, and Gautier continued, 'Have you been to the hotel where your nephew was living?'

'Not as yet. I plan to go this afternoon.'

122

'I will arrange for you to be taken there. In the meantime, you have had a long journey and must be tired. I am sure you would prefer not to stay here talking in these depressing surroundings.' Gautier pointed at the drab green walls of his office.

'What alternative do you suggest, Monsieur?'

'I usually take my lunch at a small café not far from here. Why do we not lunch there together?'

'I could not possibly impose on you.'

'You would be doing me a favour, Madame. As a single man I eat almost all of my meals alone, and to have you as a guest would be a rare pleasure.' Gautier could see that Madame Lupin was still hesitant, so he added, 'The matters we have to discuss will, I am sure, bring unhappy memories. Let us at least discuss them in congenial surroundings.'

'You are a persuasive man.' Madame Lupin smiled. 'Very well, I accept your invitation.'

Once again, the café in Place Dauphine was peacefully sleepy and, on a day that had been growing oppressively warm, its shadowy interior was inviting. As always, its clientele was mixed: *petits fonctionnaires* from the Palais de Justice, a few young advocates not yet affluent enough to afford good restaurants, and a handful of boatmen from the Seine who had discovered the café when it first opened several years previously and used it as a kind of club.

'As you can see, this is an unpretentious place,' Gautier told Madame Lupin when they reached the café, 'but one can usually rely on the cuisine.'

'That need not embarrass you, Monsieur. We Armands from Bergerac are also unpretentious, although my poor nephew may have given you a different impression. My brother, his father, came from a family of blacksmiths and my late husband was a small grocer.'

'In that case, neither of them would have been well-disposed to my father. He was a country tax collector.'

Madame Lupin laughed, and they ordered their meal together. As they were drinking their aperitifs, she looked at Gautier and asked him bluntly, 'Am I allowed to know how my nephew died?'

'He was murdered with a bomb.'

'Yes. The police told me as much, but I wish to know more: the circumstances of his death, any events which may have led up to it and your opinion of who might have murdered him.'

'The facts are plain enough, but as to my opinion' – Gautier shrugged – 'an investigation has only just been begun.'

He decided to tell her everything he knew about de Périgord's murder, beginning with the cobra which had been found in his bed at the Hôtel Meurice. Madame Lupin did not flinch as he described how Yvette had died, how the snake had been decapitated and the grisly wreckage of the *calèche* in the Bois de Boulogne. Her frail appearance, Gautier realized, must conceal exceptional resources of inner strength.

'So the poor boy was right after all,' she said sadly after Gautier had finished.

'You mean when he told you his life was in danger?'

'How do you know he did?'

'We found a letter you had written to him among his belongings. It was by reading it that we found out you were his only remaining relative.'

'Poor Frédé! Even as a small boy he used to believe that he was constantly threatened, that other boys were conspiring against him, that he was alone against the world. We used to dismiss his fears as the fancies of too vivid an imagination, but now I wonder whether they may not have been a premonition of how his life was to end.'

Madame Lupin took a handkerchief from her reticule and blew her nose. Gautier sensed that this was the only sign she would give of the emotion which memories of her nephew had aroused. 'I noticed you called him "Frédé" in your letter. Was it an affectionate family nickname?'

'Not really. His Christian name was "Frédéric", which he hated. "Armand" is our family surname and he only took to using it as a first name when he came to Paris, adding "de Périgord" to lend it distinction; a silly affectation, I suppose.'

'Harmless enough. Tell me about his boyhood and his family.'

The dishes they were served that day – Potage aux Meuniers and Boudin à la Normande – were both typical of Normandy, for although the new proprietor was from the Auvergne, he had wisely decided to continue with the kind of cuisine which had been popular with the café's patrons. While the soup was being served, Madame Lupin talked about her nephew.

Frédéric had been a highly sensitive boy, she told Gautier, and spoiled by his mother, who smothered him with an obsessive love and protectiveness. He had also been a greedy boy who had become gross through overeating. At school, though, he had excelled, was good at mathematics and an excellent linguist, becoming fluent in several foreign languages, as well as showing a flair for writing poetry.

'In short, he was fat, spoilt and clever: an unattractive combination,' Madame Lupin said, 'and the other boys hated him for it. Boys can be very cruel and Frédé was teased unmercifully and bullied by older boys.'

'Which explains why he felt he was being persecuted.'

'Exactly. At an early age he decided he must learn how to protect himself. He spent hours developing his physique and took lessons in fencing and pistol shooting. The boys soon stopped calling him "Frédé the *pédé*" and other mocking names.'

'Was he homosexual?'

'Who knows? Frédé was not overtly homosexual, but he did have a very close friendship, unhealthily close one might say, with another boy younger than himself and from a very poor family. Personally, I always thought their friendship was completely innocent.'

'Did the boys remain friends?' Gautier's question was prompted by intuition rather than logic.

'Oh, yes. In fact, some months after Frédé came to Paris the boy followed him here.'

'Was his name Lucien?'

'How did you know?'

Gautier told Madame Lupin that Lucien had been living in an apartment rented by de Périgord, as much a servant as a friend. He also explained that after de Périgord's death, Lucien had suddenly packed his belongings and left the apartment.

'You are not suggesting that he killed my nephew, surely?'

'No, but one would like to know why he left so hurriedly.'

While they were eating, Madame Lupin continued talking about her nephew and his family in Bergerac. Frédé's parents had both died while he was still an adolescent, his father of consumption and his mother of typhoid. Madame Lupin and her husband, who had no children of their own, had taken the boy into their home and he had lived with them until he left Bergerac for Paris. Even while at school he had enjoyed a modest success with his writing and a local newspaper had published some of his poems and articles. So, confident that he would be able to find fame in a wider literary world, he had left home for Paris.

'My husband had died by that time,' Madame Lupin told Gautier, 'but he had left me well provided for and I was able to give Frédé a small allowance to supplement what he would earn from his writing. As you know, he needed my support for only a short time, and before long he was earning enough to live permanently in a hotel. A hotel, if you please, and one of the best in Paris!'

Gautier hoped his aunt would never have to know that de Périgord had not relied on writing to finance his style of life. His blackmailing activities may well have provided the motive for his murder, and in this case they might become known when the murderer was brought to justice. Madame Lupin was obviously fond of her nephew and one could imagine her distress should that happen.

'In your last letter to your nephew,' he said, 'you mentioned that he had been working for the Government.'

'Yes, he told me as much.'

126

'Have you any idea what kind of work that might have been?'

'No. I had the impression that it was important and therefore highly confidential.'

During the remainder of their lunch they discussed what Madame Lupin would have to do that afternoon. Gautier told her of the belongings that de Périgord had left in his suite at the hotel, his clothes, his collection of swords and his photographs. The management of the Meurice had offered to have everything packed and sent to Bergerac, but wanted Madame Lupin to inspect it first.

'The management have been very kind. They have invited me to spend tonight in the hotel at their expense so that I need not return home until tomorrow. I am hesitant about accepting their offer.'

'Don't be. The train journey is too long for you to undertake twice in one day.'

Gautier told her that he would ask Surat to accompany her to the hotel and give her all the assistance she needed. Her nephew's letters and the money he had left in the safety deposit would have to be kept by the police until the investigation of his death had been concluded. Then they would be returned to her or to whatever lawyer she appointed to settle de Périgord's estate.

'You have been very kind, Monsieur,' Madame Lupin said. 'I was dreading coming to Paris and facing the unpleasantness of dealing with poor Frédé's death, but you have been a great help and comfort.'

She talked a little longer about Frédé and his ambitions. He had come to Paris, she said, determined to achieve success so that he would be able to return home as a celebrity. Gautier was surprised at the composure with which she had accepted her nephew's death. Had she too had a presentiment, he wondered, that he might die before he could return home from his voluntary exile? When they had left the café and were walking back to Sûreté headquarters, he asked her one final question.

'Your letter to your nephew which we found in his

hotel suite was a reply to one he had written to you, was it not?'

'Yes, to the one in which he had told me that his life was in danger.'

'You did not bring that letter with you, by any chance?'

'No. You may think me silly, Inspector, but I never keep personal letters. In time, any pleasure they may have brought fades, leaving only sad memories.'

'Did he tell you why he believed his life was threatened and by whom?'

Madame Lupin shook her head. 'No, but he seemed genuinely frightened. I recall very well the words he used. "It is not the épée or the pistol shot that I fear, but a coward's knife in the back." '

Chapter 13

The Cercle Angevin was difficult to find and no doubt the club's members preferred it that way. The entrance to the building, in a small street off Rue La Boétie, was through an archway with large wooden doors which were usually kept shut. Beyond them lay a cobbled courtyard which was overlooked by the club's premises on the upper floors of the building. Some other men's clubs in Paris had imitated the clubs of English gentlemen in Pall Mall by installing white-haired uniformed porters at a desk by the entrance to repel strangers. The Cercle Angevin scorned such extravagance and was content with a traditional conciergerie manned by a lady, larger but no more attractive than the one at de Périgord's apartment building. The full name of the club was Le Cercle des Chevaliers d'Angou, but the members, deciding that it was too pretentious, had agreed to abbreviate it. The Chevaliers d'Angou was, in any case, an ancient order of chivalry which had long ago lost its significance.

When Gautier had returned to the Sûreté after lunching with Madame Lupin, he had found a message asking him to meet the Prefect of Police at the Cercle Angevin as soon as he conveniently could. He was curious to know why the Prefect should wish to see him at his club rather than in his office, which was only a short distance from Sûreté headquarters. Since it seemed unlikely that the Prefect wanted him to see the club's amenities as a possible candidate for membership, he concluded that the reason for inviting him there was to keep the meeting unofficial and confidential. When a club servant took him to a private dining-room on the third floor, he saw that his deduction had been correct. The Prefect had been lunching there with Sigmund Locke.

'I believe you have already met Chief Inspector Gautier,' he told Locke.

As they shook hands, Locke inclined his head in a slight bow. Gautier supposed that the bow must be a sign of Locke's Germanic background. Englishmen could be stiff and formal, but they seldom bowed.

The two men had been sharing a bottle of vintage port after their lunch and Locke poured a glass for Gautier. He had drunk port before, but only the insipid variety which the French took as an aperitif. The bottle of vintage port he was given now carried an English name and Locke explained that the port trade in and around Oporto had been developed almost entirely by Englishmen.

'We have invited you here, Gautier,' the Prefect said when Locke had finished his dissertation on port, 'as we wish to discuss a very delicate matter which must not go beyond the three of us.'

'Does it concern the death of Monsieur Armand de Périgord?' Gautier asked, and the other two men looked at him sharply and then at each other.

'It does,' the Prefect replied, 'but only indirectly.'

'When you came to see Monsieur Locke at the Ritz Hotel the other day,' the Prefect continued, 'I understand you said you wished to talk to Madame Locke. Would you tell us why?'

Now Gautier understood the purpose behind this clandestine meeting. Locke had somehow found out that his wife was secretly meeting de Périgord and had immediately packed her off to England. Now he wished to know whether Gautier knew of her assignations and if so how much. Gautier supposed he could have parried the question diplomatically, for Locke might prefer not to know what the night porter at the Meurice had told him, but he decided it was better to be frank. Locke gave the impression of being a man who liked direct answers.

'I have been given to believe that Madame Locke was

130

meeting Armand de Périgord secretly,' he said.

'When and where?'

'At night in the hotel.'

'How could you possibly know that, Gautier?' the Prefect asked.

'I fear it is true,' Locke said, 'but how did you find out?'

'A hotel servant saw her going to his bedroom late at night.'

Locke's face, normally composed and grave, seemed for one brief instant to sag in despair, and Gautier understood why. The man had married a young and beautiful girl and had been forced to watch as she was unfaithful to him. No doubt, he must have known of her affair with the Prince of Wales in England.

'How many people know about this?' he asked Gautier.

'Only the man who saw her.' Gautier's reply was truthful. Henri, the night porter, had told Yvette what he had seen, but Yvette was dead.

'What can be done about him?' Locke asked the Prefect.

'You may be confident, Monsieur, that he will tell no one else,' Gautier said.

'Would money help? I am prepared to go to any lengths to make sure this man remains silent.'

'I am sure we can rely on Gautier to handle things,' the Prefect said quickly. He may have detected, as Gautier had, a sinister implication in Locke's remark. 'What seems to be equally important is the wider issue of de Périgord's death, which the Sûreté is investigating. I assume that there can be no question of Madame Locke's name being brought into that?'

'How could it be?' Locke demanded. 'She was in England when he was murdered.'

'Perhaps it would be helpful if I told you gentlemen about the enquiries I have been making. From what we know so far, it is apparent that de Périgord was a blackmailer.'

'So, it was he who was blackmailing the Comtesse de Chartres!' the Prefect exclaimed.

131

Gautier told them that among de Périgord's papers he had found evidence which showed that he had been blackmailing at least two women and may well have been planning to trap a third into a situation where she would be vulnerable to extortion. Nothing had been found to link Madame Locke's name with his.

'From what we know of de Périgord's behaviour,' he concluded, 'it is likely that given time he would have found a way of compromising her as well.'

'How long ago did Madame Locke meet him?' the Prefect asked Locke.

'I have been thinking about that. They must have first met at a soirée at the home of Comtesse Greffulhe, to which we were invited during our last visit to Paris some three weeks ago.'

'Did she see de Périgord again during that visit?'

'She may have done, but only briefly. We returned to London soon afterwards,' Locke replied, and he added angrily, 'Now I know why she persuaded me to stay at the Hôtel Meurice on this trip. She complained that the ambience at the Ritz was too formal. Too formal, indeed! I should never have given in to her.'

'From what you have told us, Gautier,' the Prefect said, 'even if de Périgord's unsavoury exploits are made public when his murderer is brought to trial, there appears to be no reason why Madame Locke's name should even be mentioned.'

'On the surface, that would seem to be so.'

'You are not intending to question her if and when she returns to Paris?'

'No, Monsieur.'

Gautier might have added that he gave the assurance without prejudicing the right to change his mind should other facts come to light. He did not, because the Prefect of Police would know that giving any such blanket indemnity was impossible in criminal cases.

'I believe we have taken matters as far as we can for the present,' the Prefect told Locke.

'I agree,' Locke turned to Gautier, 'and I would like to

thank you, Inspector, for your frankness. My position is extremely difficult and if you can keep my wife's name out of any scandal that may develop, rest assured you will be well rewarded.'

'I will escort you to your carriage,' the Prefect told Locke.

As the two men left the room, Gautier heard the sound of horses' hooves from outside. Looking out of the window, he saw that a carriage had been driven through the archway into the courtyard below. The black Victoria was beautifully appointed, its bronze fittings gleaming, its wheels immaculately clean. He could see that, as Duthrey had told him, the coachman was also black, a smiling negro dressed in dark blue livery.

When the Prefect returned, he said to Gautier cheerfully, 'There's some port left in that decanter. Why don't we continue indulging ourselves in the English fashion?' He refilled their glasses, and then remarked, 'I suppose you have never visited my club before. As you can see, it is not so lavish as some others in Paris, but it possesses some advantages which others do not.' He smiled. 'Apart from anything else, we are within walking distance of the Elysée Palace.'

The remark was no doubt intended to tell Gautier something, and he was sure he would find out what it was in due course. So he made no comment. The Prefect continued, 'You will have realized that the reason I asked you to meet Sigmund Locke here was to guarantee secrecy. The matter which we discussed could have repercussions of national importance.'

'Presumably, if Monsieur Locke's bank is involved, it must be a matter of finance.'

'It is. Our Government is at present negotiating a massive loan, which is being underwritten by Locke's bank. Until the details are settled and the loan agreed, it is imperative that its purpose and scale should not be made public. I will tell you, but please treat the information as confidential. You should tell nobody, not even any of your colleagues in the Sûreté.'

133

The purpose of the loan, he explained, was twofold: firstly, to enable France to buy the patent of a new and deadly machine-gun which had just been developed in a central European country; the second stage would be to put the gun into mass production as quickly as possible.

'No weapon in the world,' the Prefect said, 'can match this gun for firepower and reliability. Possession of it would give our army a superiority over all others, including that of Germany.'

So that was it, thought Gautier. The German bogey again. Although more than three decades had passed since the humiliation of the war with Prussia, successive French Governments were still obsessed with Germany and with the importance of revenge. The pride of France demanded it. Gautier himself had more than once come into contact with representatives of international armament manufacturers who were trying to exploit France's hunger for military power and for revenge on Germany. They had infiltrated Paris society and, using the resources of their firms, intrigued to buy favours from Government ministers and people of influence.

'Are you saying, Monsieur,' he asked the Prefect, 'that any scandal involving Madame Locke could endanger these negotiations?'

'That may seem strange to you, but it well could. Let me explain. This would not be the first time that Madame Locke has brought embarrassment on her husband.'

'Because she was thought to have been the mistress of the Prince of Wales?'

'You have heard that story, then?' The Prefect sighed. 'Whether it is true or not I cannot say, but it caused a minor sensation in London. Edward, as you may know, has been strongly criticized, not only for his string of mistresses, but for having friends – actors, racing men, money-lenders – who the English felt should not be admitted to society.'

'But even supposing that Madame Locke's name was linked with that of de Périgord, why should that affect the Government's negotiations with Locke's bank? We

French are much more liberal than the English in matters of morality.'

'It would, if for no other reason, because it would focus public attention on Locke and therefore on the loan. Rumours would fly. Questions would be asked in the Chambre des députés.'

The Prefect explained that the Government did not need the authority of Parliament to contract a loan, even one of the size required, but opposition in the Chambre des députés would make its negotiation much more difficult, if not impossible. More serious than that, any public scandal would attract the attention of other countries which might also wish to acquire the new gun.

'Now you can understand,' the Prefect concluded, 'why Madame Locke's name must be kept out of this business.'

'Yes, Monsieur. That should not be impossible, unless, of course, we discover that she was in some way implicated in de Périgord's death.'

'That's inconceivable! A ridiculous idea!'

'I have one question to ask if I may. De Périgord led his aunt to believe that he was doing important work for the Government. Do you know anything of that?'

'Actually, he has done work for the Government.' The Prefect hesitated, giving the impression that he was reluctant to tell Gautier any more. 'This new gun has been developed by an armament firm in a central European country. De Périgord was one of the few people in France who spoke the language of that country, and so he was employed as an interpreter during early discussions with the firm. One could scarcely call that important Government work, could one?'

'But secret work?'

'Yes. I can tell you that we were worried about de Périgord. The man obviously had far more money than he could have earned from writing and interpreting. We had been considering the possibility that he might be selling information about the machine-gun to a foreign power. Finding out that he was no more than a common blackmailer is reassuring.'

135

'Not to the ladies he was blackmailing, I imagine.'

'I suppose not. Anyway, he is dead now, and I am sure I can rely on you to bring the investigation into his death to a speedy conclusion.'

The finality in the Prefect's remark made it plain that the meeting was at an end. His wishes, or rather those of the Government, had been made clear, and the onus was now on Gautier to comply with them. The secrecy of the meeting was also a subtle indication that he should tell no one of what had taken place, not even the Director General of the Sûreté. It was not the first time that Gautier had been placed in such a position and, while it was reassuring to know that he had the confidence of the Prefect, there might be difficulties ahead.

As they were walking down the stairs together, the Prefect remarked, 'At least the murder of this man de Périgord will resolve Madame Becker's problems.'

'Yes. One hopes that will be the end of the blackmail threats.'

The Prefect smiled. 'But not of your English lessons, I trust.'

'We shall have to see.'

When they reached the street, Gautier began looking for a fiacre. 'Are you returning to your office, Monsieur?' he asked the Prefect.

'No, I have an appointment.' Again the Prefect smiled. 'Within walking distance and in a different direction.'

Gautier remembered an earlier remark which the Prefect had made. The President's palace was only a short walk away. Was the Prefect now hinting that he was going to have an audience with the President? And if so, was it to report on their meeting with Sigmund Locke? That Madame Locke's reputation had become a matter of national importance seemed too bizarre, unless of course Gautier had not been told the whole story.

As he was being driven back to the Sûreté, he found himself thinking about Locke. Twice during the meeting, the Englishman had hinted that he would be prepared to dispense money to get what he wanted. Wealthy people,

Gautier knew, often appeared to believe that money could buy anything and anybody, and Locke had also given an impression of a ruthless determination to achieve his ends which many people might find menacing.

The news which he received when he reached Sûreté headquarters suggested that the Prefect's confidence in an early solution to de Périgord's murder was premature. Lucien had vanished. Either he had left Paris, or had gone to ground in the shadowy world inhabited by small-time criminals and apaches, in which a man with the right credentials could easily lose his identity and disappear. To find him, the police would need to activate their small army of informers and that might take several days, if not weeks.

Enquiries which had been made among the potential bomb makers of Paris had been only slightly less dis-appointing. Three of those on the suspect list had died and one had gone to Marseilles, where he was under police surveillance as a possible member of a gang of bank robbers. So far, only two men had been identified whom the local police believed might still sometimes be involved in criminal activities. One, a former anarchist named Korsokov, was claiming now to have been converted to the Muslim faith and was thought to be supplying forged papers and weapons to Africans entering France illegally. Dumas, the other suspect, had been a soldier until he was dismissed from the army, unjustly he claimed. To take his revenge, he had planted bombs in two military barracks and at the Ministry of War, and had been sent to the penal colony in New Caledonia for ten years. Now returned, he was working as a mechanic for a gas company. No evidence had yet been found that either man had been involved in the murder of de Périgord.

Gautier began going through the reports that had accumulated on his desk during the morning, rereading some, putting others aside to be incorporated in his own report for the Director General. He had not started work on the report when a messenger brought him a handwritten note which had been handed in downstairs. The note read:

Monsieur Gautier,

I have information of the greatest importance concerning the murder of Monsieur Armand de Périgord. Since I do not wish to be seen entering police premises at the present time, please be kind enough to come and speak to me in private. I shall wait for you in my carriage outside Notre Dame.

Elizabeth Deslandes

As he went downstairs, Gautier reflected that this was yet another incident to remind him of Claire Ryan. He had already had one reminder when Catriona Becker had taken him to walk in Parc Monceau. Not long ago, Claire had come to the Sûreté to see him, but had been reluctant to enter the building and they had talked on the embankment by the Seine.

Madame Deslandes's carriage was the only one standing in the small square in front of Notre Dame cathedral, and the coachman was standing by it, obviously looking out for someone. When Gautier told the man who he was, he opened the door for him to climb into the carriage. The blinds had been pulled down, and inside, in the gloom, Madame was sitting, very upright but not this time wearing a veil.

'Thank you for coming so promptly, Inspector,' she said as Gautier sat down opposite her.

'How can I help you, Madame?'

She was not, as Gautier had seen from her portrait, a beautiful woman, but her face, with its imposing forehead and aquiline nose, had dignity. One could imagine her in an evening gown walking down a grand staircase in some ambassador's residence, elegantly and with style. This afternoon, though, her eyes were red and swollen, her cheeks sagging with weariness and her mouth trembled as she spoke.

'It is I who can help you, Inspector. You see, I know who murdered Monsieur Armand de Périgord.'

'Are you certain?'

'Oh, yes. The murderers are two ladies whom you know, the Comtesse de Chartres and Madame Becker.'

'Madame, I was with Madame Becker on the evening and at the very time that Monsieur de Périgord was killed.'

'That may be so. I am not suggesting that these two ladies actually killed him, but they conspired to have him murdered.'

'But what possible reason could they have for wanting him killed?'

'Revenge.' The eyes of Madame Deslandes filled with tears, and Gautier could sense that she was restraining her sobs. 'Both these ladies had been poor Armand's mistresses and they were furious when I supplanted them in his affections.'

'That would scarcely seem to be a motive for murder.'

'Why not? You have been studying English, Inspector, so you should know that the English have a saying about the fury of a woman scorned.'

'Have you any proof of this?'

'Work it out for yourself, Inspector. That bomb can only have been planted in Armand's carriage by someone who knew him well, knew his habits and where he would be dining that evening. I leave it to you to find what additional proof you need.' Madame Deslandes paused, a mounting indignation reinforcing her grief. 'Indeed, there may well have been a third woman in the conspiracy, and one of my closest friends at that. Madame Léontine Colbert.'

'Why do you suspect her?'

'Because it must have been an admirer of hers, her husband's assistant, who planted the bomb.'

Chapter 14

The streets were almost empty when Gautier left his apartment on the Left Bank and began walking to Sûreté headquarters. Another hour would pass before the suppliers of provisions – milk, vegetables, meat – would arrive with their carts and begin shouting their traditional cries, attracting the cooks from bourgeois homes to come out and make their purchases for the day. A coach similar to the one owned by Madame Deslandes passed him, the coachman apparently asleep, allowing the horses to find the way home. Inside the coach, a white-haired man in evening dress was slumped against the cushions, also asleep. One could only speculate on what nocturnal adventures could have lasted so long and left him exhausted. The only other vehicle in the street was an empty hearse on its way to load up with its melancholy burden in good time for the procession to the church. Was the hearse an omen, Gautier wondered, of more violence and death to come?

He was walking to work at a leisurely pace because he felt he needed to marshal his thoughts and to plan the day ahead. By coming to see him the previous afternoon, Madame Deslandes had introduced another complication into an already involved case of murder. Gautier was inclined to dismiss her accusations against Madame Becker and the Comtesse de Chartres as the hysterical fantasies of a woman deranged by grief, for she had offered no solid evidence to substantiate them. Even so, her mention of the name of Colbert's assistant, Emil Bey, was a reminder to Gautier that he should not arrive at any premature conclusions about de Périgord's murder. Bey had been evasive and shifty when he had been questioned about the cobra and may well have been lying. The time had come, Gautier decided, to review all he knew about an affair which had already encompassed two deaths, a suicide and two cases of blackmail.

When he arrived at his office, he read the reports on the previous day's enquiries. There was still no news of Lucien, but when he had visited de Périgord's *garçonnière*, Surat had found an envelope full of assorted photographs. Most of them had been taken in the apartment and looked as though they may have been de Périgord's first experiments with a camera, using whatever subjects were at hand. Among them were photographs of the concierge, who must have been persuaded reluctantly to face the camera. Another was of a man wearing a coachman's livery and carrying a whip.

Gautier was studying the photograph, which he realized must be one of Lucien, when a messenger came into the office bringing a visitor who had arrived to see him. It took Gautier a few seconds to recognize Luc Deslandes, for the Ambassador's son had shaved off his beard since their last meeting. All army officers wore beards, and in some regiments an officer wishing to remove his beard, whatever the reason, was obliged to obtain his commanding officer's permission to do so. Now that Luc had left the army, he was freed of these constraints.

'I apologize for disturbing you so early in the day, Inspector, but I felt it was essential that I should speak with you as soon as possible.'

'I am at your disposal, Monsieur.'

The Ambassador's son appeared to be in a more affable mood than he had been in his mother's house, which might mean that he had come to ask a favour.

'I only heard last night that my mother had been to see you.' Gautier said nothing, so Luc continued, 'Inspector, you must forget that she was ever here. You have to appreciate that she has been under a tremendous strain.'

'That is understandable, Monsieur.'

141

'Then take no notice of what she told you. How could she possibly believe that the Comtesse de Chartres would wish to have this man de Périgord murdered? That is what she told you, was it not?'

'She did, and made the same accusation against Madame Catriona Becker.'

'I know nothing of Madame Becker, but the Comtesse has been a close friend of our family for years. What possible reason could she have for having this man murdered?'

'Your mother claims that it was vengeance; that he had broken off his affair with the Comtesse in favour of her.'

'What! Everyone in Paris knows that the man was a *pédé*.' Deslandes jumped to his feet and began striding up and down the office, waving his arms agitatedly. 'Can't you see, Inspector? This is just a delusion. How could my mother have had an affair with de Périgord? The only explanation can be that her mind became quite unbalanced after my father's death. Why, she scarcely knew the man!'

Madame Deslandes and de Périgord, Luc told Gautier, may have met once or twice, but nothing more than that. De Périgord had never come to his family's home. Luc was certain of that.

'If they had been having an affair, where would they have had their assignations? In a hotel? It isn't credible.'

'De Périgord had a *garçonnière* in Rue des Moines,' Gautier told him. 'We know that other women visited him there.'

'Then you must know whether my mother did. Have you any evidence at all to support what she is claiming?'

'No. I admit we have none.'

'There you are! As I say, she is suffering from delusions. And as for the Comtesse de Chartres, surely no one could believe that she planted the bomb that killed this man?'

'Of course not, but she might have hired someone to do it.'

'Who? Tell me, who could she have found to do it?'

Gautier shrugged. 'One could find plenty of people in

142

Paris who would murder if the price were right.'

'With a bomb? The bomb is a sophisticated weapon and difficult to handle.'

'Even so, there are people in the criminal world who have the skill needed to make one.'

'Former anarchists, I suppose? I am surprised that there are any of them left. It must be more than ten years since the last anarchist bomb exploded.'

'Some of them are former anarchists, but there are others as well.'

'Have you established whether any of them might be involved in the murder of de Périgord?'

'Not as yet. Our enquiries are continuing.'

Deslandes had made his point and seemed to have nothing constructive to add to what he had said. His final remark before he left Gautier's office was, 'I refuse to believe for one moment that the Comtesse de Chartres was in any way involved in this business. I shall speak to my mother and persuade her to admit that her accusations were just a wild invention.'

Soon after Deslandes had left, Gautier held a conference in his office. The investigation into de Périgord's murder was, in his view, becoming too diffuse, with time and energy being spent on following leads which might have only an indirect relevance to the case. In such a situation, a meeting of all the police officers involved, with an exchange of views and impressions, could often sharpen the focus and identify the best direction to take. He had left a message for Surat earlier that morning, asking him to assemble the officers he needed, and presently they arrived. Apart from Surat himself and two junior officers who had been working on the case, there was an inspector named Giraud, who had a long experience of dealing with the lower criminal elements in Paris.

They began by reviewing progress, and came to the conclusion that so far it had been disappointing. The only significant achievement had been finding the photograph of Lucien. Surat had arranged for copies of this to be made and he distributed them at the meeting.

'The man Laborde who is suspected of putting that snake in de Périgord's bed is also as far as we know a coachman,' Inspector Giraud remarked. 'Are we then looking for two coachmen?'

'It is possible that Lucien and Laborde are the same person,' Surat said. 'I shall take the photograph round to the Hôtel Meurice and see whether any of the staff recognize him.'

'If they do, that would mean that this Lucien has been masquerading as Laborde. What reason could he have for putting the snake in his master's bed?'

'One can think of no reason unless they had quarrelled over the division of the money they were making out of blackmail.'

Though he had told Surat of them, Gautier had not mentioned de Périgord's blackmailing activities in his reports for the Director General. Madame Becker had told him in confidence that she was being blackmailed, and it was only now, when the discovery of the photograph of her and of the Comtesse de Chartres had proved irrefutably that de Périgord had been implicated, that he was prepared to make it part of the murder enquiry. He gave the men at the meeting a summary of what she had told him.

'So, the number of people who might have wished de Périgord dead grows,' Giraud said. 'We have the husbands of the women he may have seduced as well as the two ladies he was blackmailing. Nor, it seems, should we rule out this character Emil Bey.'

'Why Bey?' Surat asked.

'Did you not form the impression when we talked to him that he was devoted to Madame Colbert?' Gautier asked. 'And not with the devotion that Plato would have recommended?'

'De Périgord's servant, Lucien, should be able to answer many of our questions.'

'I agree. Finding him must be our first priority,' Gautier said. He turned to Giraud. 'Would you be willing to use your informers?'

144

Over the years, Inspector Giraud had built up a formidable army of police informers in the Paris underworld. He used them only sparingly, because every time he did he exposed them to danger. Anyone discovered to be helping the *flics* had a short expectation of life.

'Are we prepared to spend money?' Giraud asked. 'Is de Périgord worth it?'

'The authorities are anxious to have this case solved as soon as possible,' Gautier replied. 'For political reasons.'

After further discussion, the meeting agreed that from then on the enquiry into de Périgord's death should concentrate on two main objectives. The first would be to find Lucien, and the second, pursued in parallel, would be to establish the identity of the person who had made the bomb.

Gautier was summarizing these conclusions when Courtrand came into the room. Everyone looked at him in surprise. Courtrand seldom entered any office in Sûreté headquarters other than his own. He believed that his should be the centre of operations, to which officers and clerks from all over the building should be summoned at his whim. Today one could tell he was in an unusually affable mood.

'Gautier, Giraud, Messieurs, I see that you are hard at work. Very commendable! And what may I ask is the purpose of this meeting?'

'We are reviewing progress in the de Périgord affair, Monsieur le Directeur.'

'Ah, truly a puzzling case! So many people might have wished that creature dead! Well, Messieurs, you need trouble your brains no longer. I know the name of the man who had de Périgord killed. He has admitted it.'

'And who was that?' Gautier knew that someone was expected to give Courtrand his cue.

'Comte Edmond de Chartres.'

Although Courtrand had given the impression that he himself had solved the de Périgord murder with some master stroke of deduction, the truth was more prosaic.

At a private dinner party in the Jockey Club the previous evening, the Comte de Chartres had boasted of having arranged for a bomb to be planted in de Périgord's carriage while he was dining in the Bois de Boulogne. He had discovered, so he had told the other dinner guests, that de Périgord had seduced his wife and had been her lover, the lover about whom all Paris had been speculating for several months. The conventional remedy would have been for him to challenge the seducer to a duel and kill him, but de Périgord was of inferior birth. No gentleman of aristocratic lineage could demean himself by fighting him. So the Comte had hired an assassin to get rid of the man.

The dinner at the Jockey Club had been held in honour of the English banker, Sigmund Locke, and what the Comte had not known was that one of the other guests was the Prefect of Police. The Prefect had told Courtrand what the Comte had said and left it to him to take what action he thought was needed.

'Do you wish to have the Comte brought in for questioning?' Gautier had asked him.

'I have already arranged for him to be arrested,' Courtrand had replied. 'A police waggon is now on its way to his home. He will be held in prison until a *juge d'instruction* has been appointed to examine him. These aristocrats must not suppose that they will be treated differently from a common criminal.'

After Courtrand had made his announcement that morning, Gautier had abandoned his conference, for he could see no reason to prolong it. At the same time, he found it hard to believe that the Comte de Chartres could have engineered de Périgord's death. Comte Edmond was all bravado, ready to make empty gestures in defence of what he thought was his honour, but he had shown no signs of the ruthlessness that would be required to organize a callous murder. His admission might seem to have brought a simple and speedy conclusion to a complex crime, but Gautier's instincts had taught him to distrust convenient solutions. He could not help wondering whether the Comte may have been drinking when he made his boast at the Jockey Club.

For the remainder of the morning he supervised the preparation of the papers that the *juge d'instruction* would need to be given before he began his examination of the Comte the following day. The information to be put into the dossier was scanty, limited as yet to little more than the facts of de Périgord's death. There would be more papers to come: the statements of witnesses and of the police officers who had been sent to the scene of the crime. As these accumulated and were supplemented by transcripts of each day's interrogations, the dossier would become formidable, comprising in all probability scores of documents.

He and Surat worked together, sending documents downstairs to be typed on the new American machines that had recently been acquired. It was a lengthy process, but by early in the afternoon they had three complete sets of papers ready, one to be sent up to the Director General and another to be passed on, once it had been approved, to whatever judge was appointed to carry out the examination.

After Surat had left, Gautier began thinking again about the way in which the de Périgord affair was developing. The dossier they had prepared would be an adequate basis for the judge to start his examination, but they gave no mention of the blackmailing of Catriona Becker and the Comtesse de Chartres. If the Comte had arranged for de Périgord to be murdered, it may well have been that he had found out about the blackmail and about de Périgord's photograph of his wife. If so, then this would surely emerge during his examination. Gautier would have liked to speak to the Comtesse on the matter, but if he questioned her at this stage he might be thought to be usurping the function of the *juge d'instruction*.

Blackmail commonly led to violence. A desperate victim might see no way of escaping except by murdering the blackmailer. But neither Catriona Becker nor the Comtesse appeared to have been desperate. Their attitude

147

to the blackmailer's demands had been almost light-hearted, and they had readily handed over the money for which they had been asked. That in itself was cause for suspicion.

It was possible, but by no means certain, that the next day's examination would provide answers to these questions, but Gautier did not enjoy the prospect of brooding over them until then. Then he had an idea. He remembered Catriona telling him that the packet of money she had left in the Bois de Boulogne had been addressed to a hotel. She could not recall which hotel, but thought it had been named after a poet or playwright. The Sûreté kept a list of all Paris hotels in alphabetical order, so he went to the general office and consulted it. He found several hotels which might have fitted her description: Hôtel Ronsard, Hôtel Victor Hugo, Hôtel de Musset, Hôtel Racine and two hotels named after Molière. Most of the hotels were in areas probably too fashionable to be used by a blackmailer, but one Hôtel Molière was in the 12th *Arrondissement*, not far from the Gare de Lyon. It was also not far from the hotel in which the printer Buisson had died of apoplexy. Gautier decided, on no more than an impulse, to visit the hotel. Even should his hunch be proved wrong, after a morning spent on paperwork he would be glad to be out of the office and working as a policeman again.

The hotel was in a shabby street near the railway station and its entrance was a narrow staircase between shops. In a tiny lobby at the top of the staircase, the proprietor was sitting behind a counter waiting for clients to arrive. He was a bulky individual with mean eyes slitting a bloated face, and although he was in his shirt-sleeves, he wore, incongruously, a red bowler hat.

Gautier told the man who he was and then, wasting no time on preliminaries, said, 'I am here in connection with a murder enquiry.'

'I know nothing of any murder, Inspector. We allow no violence in this hotel.'

'Very possibly, but I have reason to believe that your

hotel has been used by a man who was recently involved in a case of blackmail.'

'Are you saying that this man was lodging here?'

'Not necessarily. He may only have been using the hotel as an address; to have mail or parcels delivered here, for example.'

The proprietor shook his head. 'That's not possible. If anyone were doing that I would know about it.'

'We believe that not many weeks ago at least one package and possibly two were brought here by hand.'

'For whom?'

'No name was written on the package; just three crosses in red ink.'

The slit eyes blinked, convincing Gautier that the man knew of the parcels, but an admission would have to be prised out of him. 'If any parcels like that were brought here, I did not see them.'

'I should think again if I were you, my friend. Think carefully. Those parcels contained money obtained by blackmail. You could be charged with conspiring to blackmail.'

The hotelier made a derisive snort. As a gesture of defiance it was not convincing. 'You do not frighten me, Inspector.'

'Perhaps not, but if you refuse to co-operate, you will be put out of business.'

'How can you do that? I have committed no offence.'

'Within an hour of my leaving here a police officer will be stationed outside the hotel, permanently. Do you suppose the *putains* will bring their clients here when they see a *flic* by the door?'

'That's outrageous!'

'Why? Allowing your hotel to be used for immoral purposes is against the law, as you well know.'

The hotelier swore, using an obscenity which probably only street girls and *flics* would understand. Gautier recognized capitulation.

'Very well. A package of the type you describe was delivered here.'

149

'Only one?'

'Two, then. But they were brought here without my consent.'

'I will pretend I believe that, but only if you tell me who collected the packages.'

'I hardly know the man. He has been here once or twice with girls, that's all.'

Gautier had brought a copy of the photograph of Lucien with him and he showed it to the hotelier. 'Could this be the man?'

'Yes. That's him all right. He calls himself Laborde.'

Chapter 15

That evening, Gautier dined alone in a small restaurant near Les Halles which catered mainly for porters from the markets nearby. For some weeks, he had been using the restaurant in the evenings as an alternative to the café in Place Dauphine, partly for the sake of variety and partly as a kind of supplement to his English lessons. Some of the many Americans who came to visit Paris had 'discovered' Les Halles. They would come there in the late evenings to drink onion soup in the cafés and mingle with the porters, believing that in this way they were seeing the real Paris. The porters accepted their presence and their curiosity with good humour, commenting on them among themselves in slang which the Americans did not understand and which would have scandalized them if they did.

Gautier was not enjoying his meal there that evening, not on account of the food which, as always, was plain but good and plentiful, but because of his mood. Finding out that de Périgord's servant Lucien and the man who called himself Laborde were the same person had given him no satisfaction, for it posed a number of questions. That afternoon, Surat had taken the photograph of Lucien to the Hôtel Meurice and the staff there had confirmed that he had been the man with plumber's tools who had borrowed the passkey in the corridor outside de Périgord's suite. What reason could Lucien have had for smuggling the snake into his master's bed? Surat had also been told that Lucien had called at the hotel during the afternoon after de Périgord's death and had been devas-

151

tated when he had been told of his death. If he had been implicated in the murder, why would he have gone to the hotel and asked for de Périgord? Gautier realized that these and other questions would have to be answered and that the answers were not likely to materialize at the *juge d'instruction*'s examination next morning.

He had just finished his meal and was brooding over his dissatisfaction, when he noticed that a group of porters sitting opposite him were looking towards the door of the restaurant with sudden interest. He turned round and saw that Catriona Becker had come in and was looking round the room. When she saw him, she came straight to his table, calling out his name.

'How did you find me?' he asked her.

'For a girl who was brought up stalking deer on the hills it was not difficult,' Catriona replied as she sat down opposite him. 'You're a creature of habit, Jean-Paul.'

What she said was true. Gautier ate in the same restaurants, more often than not ordered the same dishes, met his friends in the same café, walked to and from work by the same route. Sometimes he told himself he did it so the Sûreté could reach him at any time, night or day. At other times, he suspected that it was simply laziness.

'I am sorry to intrude on your bachelor evening, but I had to see you.'

'No need to apologize. May I order you something?'

'Thank you, no. I have already dined.' Although she appeared to be in good spirits, Gautier thought he could detect the tension of anxiety in her eyes. Her next remark showed the reason for it. 'I suppose you know that Edmond de Chartres has been arrested.'

'Yes. He has been telling people that he was responsible for Armand de Périgord's murder.'

'Do you believe him?'

'Let me put it this way, I would need a good deal of convincing before I did.'

'It's totally unbelievable! Absurd!'

'We will soon learn the truth. He is to appear before a *juge d'instruction* in the morning.'

Catriona hesitated before she asked her next question.

'As part of his examination, the judge will study all the evidence relating to the murder, is that not so?'

'Yes. I spent this afternoon assembling it.'

'Will that photograph of me be part of the evidence?'

Now Gautier understood her anxiety. 'I would hope not,' he replied. 'De Périgord's blackmailing of you would not appear to have provided a motive for the Comte to have him killed, but it will be for the judge to decide.'

He could have told her that the judges appointed to supervise the examination of a criminal offence were not usually the equal in intellect of the great legal brains who presided over the Great Assize Court in the Palais de Justice. An impartial observer might feel that they were chosen as much for their ability to ferret out the truth by tricking witnesses into making incriminating statements, as for any knowledge of the law.

'If the photograph and the story of my visit to Armand's apartment are made public, it will be the end of my engagement to Wayne,' Catriona said miserably.

'We can only hope that it will not come to that.'

'Would it be of any help if you spoke to the Prefect of Police on my behalf?'

'If you want to follow that route, it would be best for you to have a word with him yourself.'

'Then I shall.' Catriona was silent for a time, as though she were trying to decide how she could best approach the Prefect. Then she said, 'And what about Maria?'

'The Comtesse de Chartres? In her case, the situation might be more difficult. If the Comte persists in claiming that he had de Périgord murdered, the Comtesse's visits to Rue des Moines are certain to be mentioned at his trial. His advocate may well put her liaison with de Périgord in the Comte's defence, claiming that his was a crime of passion.'

'You have seen the photographs Armand took of her, then?'

'One of them. He had kept it locked in his safe deposit with the one of you.'

'Mother of God! She will be appalled!' Catriona

seemed more upset than she had when Gautier had shown her the photograph of herself. Gautier realized that she must be aware that the Comtesse had posed naked for the photographs. 'Would you be willing to tell Maria this? To warn her of what may happen?'

'I can see no reason why she should not be told. If the photograph is to be used in the Comte's defence, her lawyers will be informed.'

'Will you come with me to see her now?'

'At this time of night?'

'Yes. She will be half-expecting you. I told her that I would be looking for you.'

'Surely it can wait until tomorrow?'

'Please, Jean-Paul, let us go to her home now! Can you not imagine how she must be feeling, alone and distraught with worry?' Catriona laid a hand on Gautier's arm, pleading. 'Do it as a favour to me. My carriage is waiting outside.'

Gautier agreed. The Comte de Chartres's claim to have arranged for de Périgord to be murdered was unconvincing to say the least, and there were contradictory statements that had still to be reconciled. On top of that, he detected inconsistencies in the accounts that Catriona had given of her visits and those of the Comtesse to de Périgord's apartment. By speaking to the two women together he might get a clearer picture of the truth.

The home of the Comte and Comtesse de Chartres was in the Faubourg St Germain, that exclusive quadrilateral of land on the Left Bank, which had always been the favourite enclave of the *gratin*. Their *hôtel particulier*, one of a number in Paris which had been the homes of aristocratic families for generations, had been built around a paved courtyard, with the house on one side and stables on the other. The stables were now used as a garage for the Comte's automobile. Comtesse Maria received Madame Becker and Gautier not in either of the house's salons, but in her boudoir. She was wearing a low-cut, pale blue gown, which heightened the striking contrast between her dark hair and ivory skin.

154

As she held out her hand for Gautier to kiss, she said, 'At last we meet, Inspector. I have heard so much about you.'

'And I of you, Madame la Comtesse.'

'But nothing flattering, I am sure.'

Behind her smile was the same look that she had given Gautier when she passed him at the entrance to the home of the French Ambassador, and again it lingered. He recognized the look as one which could sometimes be seen on the faces of men as well as of women; a look not of a predator, but of a collector examining a new species and wondering whether it might be added to a collection. He had no doubt that the Comtesse had added many men to hers.

'Tell the Comtesse of the photograph of her which you found among Armand's belongings,' Catriona said to Gautier.

'Have you brought it with you?'

'No, Madame.'

'What did you think of it?' the Comtesse asked coyly.

The unexpectedness of the question disconcerted Gautier. He had thought that the mention of the photograph might cause the Comtesse if not shame, then at least some embarrassment. 'I had the impression that Monsieur de Périgord was not very skilled at photography,' he said diplomatically.

'That is true. Others have taken far better photographs of me.'

'I once saw a very fine portrait of you at the Salon d'Automne. I believe it was by Boldini.'

'Did you really like that painting? Many of my friends thought it did not do me justice.'

'You two will have to forgive me if I leave you now,' Catriona interrupted impatiently.

'Surely you are not going,' the Comtesse said.

'Yes. I only brought the Inspector here so that you two could discuss how this delicate matter could best be handled,' Catriona replied. Then she added, 'Sadly, I do not have the time to stay arguing on the merits of portraiture. I have another engagement.'

155

'At this hour?' The Comtesse's smile had no more than a touch of malice. 'Well, dear, we will not embarrass you by asking what that engagement might be.'

She tugged at a bell-pull hanging on the wall nearest her and a footman appeared to show Catriona out. Then, once they were alone, she sat down on a *chaise-longue*, reclining and leaving room for Gautier to sit at the end by her feet. Gautier suppressed a smile. The posture she had adopted might well have been a pose for a portrait by one of the lesser and more banal of artists; a society beauty with an admirer gazing up at her.

As he looked at her more closely, he could understand why the Prince of Wales had been so infatuated. She was still beautiful, even though the signs of impending age, or perhaps of a dissolute life, were beginning to show in her face. The house was lit by gas lamps which were acknowledged to be kinder to the complexion and he supposed that, when exposed to the harsher scrutiny of electricity, she would wear cosmetics.

'Now what are we going to do about this photograph?' she asked him.

'Has your husband seen it?'

'I am sure he hasn't. Why do you ask?'

'I had thought that perhaps the blackmailer might have sent a copy to him.'

The Comtesse seemed astonished by the question. 'Why on earth would he do that?'

'I assume the reason why you paid fifty thousand francs was to stop him sending it to your husband.'

'Heavens, no! I would not be particularly upset if Edmond were to see it. What could he do? No, it is my family who must on no account see that photograph. Are you aware of my background, Inspector?'

'I have heard that your father is a Spanish grandee.'

'That and more. Much more.'

She told Gautier that her father was one of the most important men in Spain and a personal friend of the king. He was also an Admiral of the Spanish fleet, a hereditary appointment, since he had never been to sea. If she were

156

known to have been photographed naked, the scandal in Madrid would be enormous and damage the family's reputation irreparably. Gautier was tempted to observe that she might have thought of the possible consequences before posing in the nude for de Périgord, but he knew from experience that sententious remarks of that kind never achieved any purpose.

'Of course it would be better if Edmond did not see the photograph. It would only wound him, or rather his vanity.'

'Could it be that he has seen it? That may be the reason why he is claiming to have had de Périgord murdered.'

'Claiming?' The Comtesse smiled. 'I can see that you do not believe his boast. Of course, he did nothing of the kind. Poor Edmond! If he ever tried to murder someone he would only bungle it.'

'Then why is he claiming that he did?'

'It's just another of his empty gestures. Edmond is obsessed with the fear that I may be having an affair. Do you know, I believe that he has been having me followed?'

'What makes you think so?'

'Once or twice I have noticed an odd little man lurking in the street outside the house at night. It was really quite comical.'

'Was Monsieur de Périgord here at the time?'

'No. On both occasions I was entertaining a group of friends – Catriona Becker, Madame Deslandes and her son, the Prefect of Police and his wife, among others. But Armand was not here. In fact, this happened after I had decided not to see him again.'

'Why did you do that? Because he was having an affair with the Ambassador's wife?'

'That was one reason. Poor Elizabeth! I was appalled when I found out. Armand was making a fool of her. Anyway, that is all in the past now. Armand is dead and we can forget about him and the blackmail.'

'You would be unwise to count on that. He may have had an accomplice.'

'You are thinking of Lucien, are you not?'

157

'So you know about Lucien?'

'I suspected that he might be involved in the blackmail. Where can I find him?'

'He has disappeared.'

'There were other photographs of me. I will find Lucien and persuade him to give them to me. I can handle Lucien.' The Comtesse may have had good reasons for her confidence. She went on, 'In the meantime, what about the photograph which you have, where is it?'

'At Sûreté headquarters.'

'Has anyone besides you seen it?'

'Not yet.'

'Then could it not disappear? You could say that you have lost it.' The Comtesse saw that Gautier would refuse, so she smiled and, without giving him time to reply, continued, 'I should not have suggested that. It was unfair of me. You and I will have to think of another solution.'

Rising from the *chaise-longue*, she went in the direction of the bell-pull and Gautier thought she was going to ring for a servant to show him out of the house. Instead, all she did was to take off the sapphire ear-rings she was wearing and place them on top of a small chest which stood against the wall. When she returned she sat down next to him.

'Poor Catriona!' she said.

'Why do you say that?'

'One could see that she left here very reluctantly.'

'I did not get that impression.'

'Oh yes. She did not want to leave us here together.'

Gautier laughed. 'Now you are being fanciful!'

'Not at all. Catriona finds you very attractive, Jean-Paul. That is why she agreed to give you lessons in English.'

'I can assure you that is not the reason.' Gautier might have told the Comtesse that Catriona had agreed to give him the lessons before she had even met him.

'Of course she finds you attractive. Any woman would.'

As she spoke she leant towards him. The movement was slow, almost imperceptible, but it brought her face closer to Gautier's, until he could scarcely avoid seeing almost all of her breasts, which were in any case generously displayed by her *décolletage*. Her taking off the earrings, he realized, had been a kind of symbolic prelude. She had a favour to ask and knew of only one currency with which she could pay for it.

'You know we are alone in the house?' she asked softly, and then laughed as she added, 'Thanks to you, my husband has been detained elsewhere.'

'It was not my decision to arrest him.' Gautier stalled, hoping he might still avoid having to rebuff her.

'Do you not think we should take advantage of the opportunity?'

'It would be most unwise.'

'Surely you do not have to leave yet? At least linger a little longer.'

'I'm sorry. I must go.'

'You do not find me attractive,' she said sadly.

'Of course I find you attractive. Any man would,' he replied, mimicking what she had said to him, flippantly so that she would not take offence.

'Very well.' The Comtesse recognized defeat. 'I will allow you to escape just this once, but do not suppose that you will be allowed to disappoint me next time.'

As he was leaving the house, Gautier admitted to himself that for a moment he had been tempted, to 'linger a little longer', as she had put it, and discover whether the rest of her body was as inviting as her breasts. He recognized, though, that her clumsy attempt to seduce him had been at best half-hearted. That might mean simply that she did not really find him attractive. On the other hand, it might equally well be that recovering her photograph was not as important to her as one might have expected.

The entrance to her house, like that of the Prefect's club, was through an archway, and as he was passing through it on his way out, Gautier thought he could hear the sound of footsteps in the street outside. Immediately he was suspicious. People who lived in Faubourg St Germain did not walk the streets at night, indeed they seldom

159

walked at any time. Could this be the little man whom the Comtesse believed her husband was employing to watch her? Alternatively, it might simply be an assassin waiting for him. He had been attacked in the street more than once.

Whoever it might be, he was approaching from the left and still some distance away. As silently as he could, Gautier slipped through the archway and across the street. Like all the streets in the Faubourg St Germain it was badly lit, and if he stood up against the wall of the house on the far side, he was confident that he would not be seen, especially as he was not wearing evening clothes and a white shirt front that would gleam in the darkness.

Presently, a man appeared, walking confidently and making no attempt to conceal his movements. He too was not wearing evening dress and it was too dark to see his face, but as he turned into the archway leading to the Comte's house, something about him seemed familiar. Only after the man had disappeared through the archway did Gautier realize why. The man's build, the slope of his shoulders, the contour of his head were identical to those of the Prefect of Police.

Chapter 16

'As I have already told you, Monsieur le Juge, my honour was at stake. His honour, his reputation, are every Frenchman's birthright and he has a moral obligation to defend them,' the Comte de Chartres said. 'This man, ignoble and worthless, had sullied my honour by seducing my wife.'

'You persist in saying that de Périgord was your wife's lover. How do you know this?'

'Everyone in Paris knows, or rather knew it.'

'Did you or anyone else ever actually discover them committing adultery?'

'The honour of great families like mine is part of France's heritage. For generations ours had remained inviolate. And then this nobody, this pathetic little scribbler from the provinces, dared to assail it. I had every right to kill him. No French court will condemn me for that.'

The examination of Comte Edmond de Chartres by the *juge d'instruction*, which had begun early that morning, had so far been a charade. One could not fault Judge Loubet. After reading the dossier, he had decided to bypass all preliminaries and go directly to the nub of the case. His task was to assemble all the available evidence and pass it to the department of the Ministry of Justice known as the Chambre des Mises en Accusations. There it would be examined by a panel of judges, who would then decide whether or not this self-professed murderer should be committed for trial.

Loubet was a kindly, patient man and his examination of the Comte had been fair, almost too fair. So far nothing had been said which would substantiate the Comte's boast that he had arranged for de Périgord to be murdered. He had refused to name the person who had thrown or planted the bomb, on the grounds that his honour would not allow him to betray his accomplice. Gautier, who was present at the examination, together with Courtrand, a junior inspector and two clerks who were recording the proceedings, almost admired the performance. The Comte had found himself thrust on to a stage where he could strut and posture before an audience who, whatever they might feel, were obliged to listen to what he chose to say. The replies he gave to Judge Loubet's questions were not answers at all, but statements, often the same statements expressed differently but always with haughty arrogance. Loubet did his best by rephrasing his questions to draw some facts from the accused, but the Comte would not be deflected from the confession he had made.

By the middle of the morning, everyone was growing restless. Courtrand had already left the hearing, explaining that he had another more important appointment. He may have been embarrassed, as he realized that his decision to arrest and imprison the Comte might have been premature. Gautier could not prevent his own attention wandering. Several times that morning he had found himself wondering about the arrival of the Prefect of Police at the home of the Comtesse late the previous night. Had the Comtesse been expecting him? If she had, it seemed unlikely that she would have invited Gautier to stay on and make love to her, unless it had been a plot to trap him in an indiscretion, which also seemed improbable.

He forced himself to listen to the judge's examination of the Comte again. The questions and answers were still following the same pattern.

'Tell us once again where you were during the evening when de Périgord was killed.'

'My wife and I were dining at the home of Madame Geneviève Straus.'

'So clearly you could not have been present when the bomb which killed de Périgord exploded.'

162

'Why should I have been? If one of my horses has to be destroyed, I employ someone to do it.'

'You are saying that you hired someone to explode the bomb?'

'Precisely.'

'Did you make the bomb yourself?'

The Comte snorted with contempt. 'What do I know of bombs or explosives? As you would expect, my military service was done in a cavalry regiment, France's finest.'

'So the man who exploded the bomb also constructed it. If you want us to believe your story you will have to name him.'

'Really, Monsieur le Juge, you cannot expect me to do that. Remember please that I am not a police informer, a common criminal. The responsibility for exterminating de Périgord is mine alone. Do you know, by the way, that his surname was really Armand? The de Périgord was an invention, a conceit of his fancy. He was the son of a blacksmith. A blacksmith, if you please!'

Before the morning was over, Judge Loubet's patience was exhausted. He told the Comte de Chartres that the examination was suspended for the time being, but that he would be required to appear for further questioning in due course. The Comte was escorted away to return to La Roquette prison, and the two clerks who had been present throughout the day left to begin preparing a verbatim transcript of the hearing.

When they were alone, Judge Loubet asked Gautier, 'What is your opinion of this affair, Gautier?'

'It is extremely complex, Monsieur; too complex in my view for us to expect a simple solution.'

'I agree with you. The Comte should not have been arrested; not at this point anyway.' What Loubet said was an implicit criticism of the Director General, but he would go no further. 'What do you suggest should be done now?'

'We need answers to a number of questions and I fear we will not find them in a judicial examination.'

'Can you give me examples?'

'I would like to know why de Périgord's servant,

Lucien, has disappeared. We cannot be certain that he did not play some part in the murder. Another question which requires answering revolves around the snake that was put into de Périgord's bed. Was it a first and unsuccessful attempt on his life? If so, who put it there?'

'You are absolutely right, Gautier,' the judge said decisively. 'This case must not be brought to a premature conclusion. We need more information and more witnesses. You must continue your investigations, and you have my authority to be absent from my examination while you do.'

When Gautier returned to his office, he found an invitation which had been delivered there earlier in the day. The invitation was for the charity gala of 'The American Wild West Show', which was to be held that evening. With the invitation came a note from Catriona Becker.

Jean-Paul,

You have already promised to join me in my patron's box this evening. A number of my friends whom you know will be there, including the Prefect of Police. We will be having supper after the performance.

Catriona

Gautier knew that he had not agreed to attend the performance of the American show, and that Catriona had done no more than hint that he might be invited. Her note could only mean that she meant to put him in a position where he could scarcely decline to attend. And to make doubly sure, she was telling him that the Prefect of Police would be there; a subtle reminder that it had been the Prefect who had asked him to help her with her blackmail problem.

The Prefect seemed to be playing a growing part in Gautier's life. He remembered how he had seen him outside the home of the Comtesse de Chartres the previous night. The memory sparked off a sudden idea. Was it

164

possible that it was the Prefect who was the Comtesse's latest lover? The remark he had made to Gautier in the Cercle Angevin showed that he knew she, as well as Catriona Becker, was being blackmailed. In his position he could not intervene to help her, but he might have devised a way of making sure that Gautier did.

The idea was intriguing. As Gautier thought about it, he could appreciate the simplicity of the plan. If he suc-ceeded in identifying who was blackmailing Catriona Becker and putting an end to his extortion, the Comtesse too would be free of her problems. On the other hand, if he were to fail, the blackmailer would blame Catriona for calling in the police and would take his revenge on her, not on the Comtesse. Should this be true, it would mean that Gautier was being used, but even so he could not help admiring the Prefect's ingenuity. He would not in any way be surprised if the Prefect were to have a mistress. A very large proportion of the married men in Paris did, and the beauty, breeding and social position of the Comt-esse would fit in very well with the Prefect's style of life.

Standing drinking by a counter was a new experience for Gautier and one which he was not sure he enjoyed. In every French café or bistro that he knew, one sat at a table, however small, and was served by a waiter, suitably dressed and suitably solicitous for one's comfort and for the *pourboire* which he knew he would be given. Making customers drink while on their feet was, he supposed, part of the legendary American efficiency. That way they would drink more, and more rapidly, and not be tempted to linger over one cup of coffee while reading a newspaper.

He had not gone to the Irish-American bar with any great expectation that he would learn anything which would help his enquiries. If nothing better, it was a way of filling in time until Surat and the other officers engaged in the investigation returned to Sûreté headquarters to make their reports. Only then would he be able to decide what further steps would need to be taken in the afternoon. Another reason for visiting the bar was the remark that Rodier, the concierge at the Meurice and a shrewd observer of people, had made about the man who had been following Armand de Périgord. The man, Rodier had said, was unmistakably French, but his manner and his dress suggested that he may have once lived in America. There was at least a slender hope that the man might frequent the Irish-American bar and that he might be known there.

When Gautier had arrived at the bar, he had found few people there. He had remembered then that a race meeting was being held at Longchamps that day. Very probably, many of the bar's regular clientele would be there, and maybe in the evening, after the last race, it might begin to fill up with racegoers. The barman who came to take his order agreed.

'They will all be in here this evening,' he told Gautier. 'Trainers, jockeys and the poor devils who have wasted their money backing some hopeless horse. In the meantime, what will you take, Monsieur?'

'A Whisky Stone Fence, if you please.'

Gautier had read in the Paris *Herald* that the Whisky Stone Fence, a combination of cider and Irish whiskey, was one of the most popular drinks served in the bar. The derivation of its name must be from racing parlance and since a stone fence must be a dangerous obstacle for a horse to jump, he assumed it carried a warning. In the event, when he tasted the drink, he found that it held none of the rich, mellow flavour of the Scotch whisky Catriona had given him.

'Do you by any chance know a Monsieur Montbrun?' he asked the barman.

'Montbrun,' the barman said thoughtfully. 'The name seems familiar. Does he go racing?'

'Not as far as I know. He is French, but dresses like an American.'

'I believe I do know the man you mean. He calls himself Theo. Works for an American firm and once spent six months in Chicago. He is always bragging about it. Comes

166

in here quite often. A funny thing, though: one never sees him talking to Americans, although we get plenty of them in here.'

'Do you know the name of his firm?'

'No. Theo has never mentioned it, even though it must have an office in Paris,' the barman replied. Then he added, 'Why don't you come back this evening? Theo often comes in at around seven for a Bourbon whiskey.'

'If I can, I will.'

'Will you take another Stone Fence?'

'I would prefer a Scotch whisky if you have one.'

As he was sipping his whisky, Gautier recalled the conversations in the Café Corneille about the invasion of Paris by Americans. His friends there were for the most part men of a liberal disposition, but they were inclined to deplore the influence which Americans and American institutions were having on life in France. He was beginning to wonder whether their disapproval was justified. It was easy to mock some of the attitudes of Americans, their veneration for money and worldly success, but in the main, those who came to visit France tried in their lives to observe precepts of honesty, industry and plain speaking, values which the cynical, hedonistic French might do well to imitate. Had the Comtesse de Chartres and Catriona Becker put principles before pleasure, they would never have become entangled in a vicious web of intrigue and deceit.

He had almost finished his whisky and was prepared to concede that his visit to the Irish-American bar had been a waste of time, when Surat arrived. He had left a message at Sûreté headquarters, as he usually did, to say where he was going, and the fact that Surat had followed him to the bar so soon told him that there must have been an unexpected development in the de Périgord affair.

'You have news for me?' he asked Surat.

'Things are beginning to happen, *patron*. First, Emil Bey has disappeared.'

'Disappeared?'

'Yes. I went to tell him that he was required to appear

before the *juge d'instruction* tomorrow, but I was told he had left the Colberts' house. It would seem that Monsieur Colbert has dismissed him.'

'Was Colbert there?'

'Yes. I spoke to him. He was in a frenzy of rage. Said he had found out that Bey had been making advances to his wife. So he threw him out.'

'Where has Bey gone, then?'

'Colbert could not say. His servants thought he may have taken the train to Marseilles, intending to return to Egypt, but Monsieur Colbert refused to discuss the matter. I have seldom seen a man so angry.'

'In that case, he will have to appear before Judge Loubet and do some explaining. See he is brought to the Palais de Justice this afternoon. You said that was your first piece of news. What is the other?'

'Dumas, the former bomb maker, is dead.'

'Dead? How did he die?'

'I understand he was shot. The police report from the 18th *Arrondissement* only came in a few minutes ago. Dumas was found dead in his apartment by neighbours.'

Chapter 17

Dumas had been living in an alley that was no more than a slit between shabby, decaying buildings. His room – one could scarcely call it an apartment – was just about large enough for a man to live and die in. His body was stretched out on the bed, as though he had just lain down for a nap or a rest, when he had been shot through the head. Whoever killed him had fired the bullet through a pillow, no doubt to deaden the sound of the shot, and the pillow had been removed and put on one side by the doctor who had examined the dead man. The body was cold, suggesting that he had been dead for several hours. There was surprisingly little blood. The doctor who had examined the body had already left to examine another in an adjoining street. That day the *quartier* was living up to its reputation for violence.

Two police officers from the 18th *Arrondissement* were on duty, one in the room, one stationed in the alley outside. Gautier asked the one in the room, 'When was the body discovered?'

'Not till almost midday, Inspector. A neighbour, a woman who comes in from time to time to clean the room, just as an act of kindness, found him.'

'Was the door locked? I assume the woman had a key.'

'Apparently she does not need one. The lock has been broken for weeks.'

Gautier and Surat looked round the room. It was tidy and clean, but hot and airless and heavy with the sickly smell of stale wine. A half-empty bottle of cheap wine and two glasses stood on a table. If Dumas had been making bombs he had removed all traces of his work. They found no tools, no wires, no explosives. Gautier was not surprised, as he had not expected to find any. With one conviction and a long prison sentence behind him, Dumas would not leave anything in the room which might implicate him in murder. He had thought they might find money, for anyone making a bomb would expect to be paid, and paid well, and people living in that *quartier* did not use banks. They found a thousand francs, hidden, but not very expertly, in one of a pair of black boots which Dumas probably wore to work. One might think that a thousand francs was not an excessive sum for helping to destroy a life but, as Gautier knew, it would be more than most working men would ever be able to amass honestly.

Leaving the policeman in the room, Gautier and Surat went down the stairs and into the alley. A small crowd had gathered outside the building and, as always, Gautier wondered why they were waiting and what they expected to see.

'Poor old Dumas!' a woman was saying. 'Who could possibly want to kill him?'

'You *flics* had better catch the scoundrel,' a man said to Gautier, 'or we will, and then heaven help the pig!'

'We can only find out who killed your friend,' Gautier told the crowd, 'if you help us. When did anyone last see him alive?'

'I saw him leaving here for work yesterday morning,' said an old man wearing a ragged cloth cap.

'And in the evening? It would seem that he had been drinking last night.'

'If he had, it was not here,' another man said. 'I was in the bistro around the corner where he went every night after finishing his meal and he never came there last night.'

'Why not ask the lady who came out of his place this morning?' an old woman in the crowd suggested.

'What lady?'

'Who knows? She was wearing a veil.'

Piece by piece, and with patient questions, Gautier extracted all the information which the onlookers could give him. Dumas had lived alone, for, although he had been married at one time, his wife had abandoned him when he had been exiled to New Caledonia. He had been popular enough, even though he rarely mixed with his neighbours in a district where there was little social life. He had been seen leaving his home for work as usual early the previous day, but no one could remember seeing him return. Only one woman had seen the lady who had called on him that morning and she lived in the room below Dumas. She had seen the lady, well-dressed and, as she had said, wearing a veil, come down the stairs and hurry into the alley outside.

'Where did she go then?' Gautier asked.

'Down the alley to the street at the bottom. I suppose she must have come in a fiacre and it was waiting for her there.'

'More likely she came in an automobile,' another man suggested. 'I saw one waiting around the corner with a chauffeur standing beside it.'

'Did you notice what colour and make it was?'

The man shook his head, but a lad in the crowd called out, 'I did. It was black, a De Dion-Bouton; the latest model.'

That afternoon, Judge Loubet decided that he would postpone any further questioning of the Comte de Chartres and go back to what appeared to be the beginning of the murder case he had been appointed to examine – the first attempt on de Périgord's life. He gave instructions that all those who could give any evidence on the death of the chambermaid Yvette in the Hôtel Meurice should be brought before him. Before questioning the other witnesses – the hotel's maids, waiters and the concierge – he wished to establish from where the cobra had been procured. Since Emil Bey had disappeared, the first witness to be called was Marcel Colbert.

At first, Colbert responded to the judge's questions

171

calmly. He conceded that the snake found in the Hôtel Meurice must be one of those he had brought back from Africa for the Institut Pasteur, but denied that he had been in any way involved in selling it to the man Laborde. That, he said, had been done without his knowledge by his assistant Emil Bey, which was the reason why Bey had been dismissed from his employ. When Judge Loubet questioned him about the statement he had made to Surat about his wife's infidelity, he began to bluster. He said indignantly that he had been mistaken and that there had never been any question of his wife having an affair with Bey or any other man.

At this point, Judge Loubet produced the note signed by 'Léontine', which Gautier had found in de Périgord's strongbox. Handing the note to Colbert, he asked him whether the handwriting was that of his wife. Colbert stared at it and intuition told Gautier that, while he had not seen it before, its message did not surprise him.

'Where did you get this?' he demanded.

'It was found in the belongings of the murdered man, Armand de Périgord.'

'Then he must have stolen it. As you can see, it is not addressed to him by name.'

'Then to whom could it have been written?'

'As to that I have no idea,' Colbert said angrily.

'But why should de Périgord have stolen it?'

'No doubt he intended to use it to blackmail my wife.'

Gautier had been listening to the cross-examination without any great interest, for he did not believe that Colbert would have any information that was relevant to de Périgord's murder. Now his suspicions were alerted. Had Colbert heard that de Périgord was a blackmailer and, if so, who had told him? One explanation might be that de Périgord had already begun to blackmail Madame Colbert before his death.

'Let us return to the matter of the snake which you brought back from Africa,' Loubet said to Colbert. 'Do you realize that it was used in an earlier attempt to kill the victim of the bomb, de Périgord?'

172

The question was not the one Gautier himself would have asked at that point, for he would have preferred to pursue the subject of blackmail. As it was, Loubet's implication that Colbert might have been in some way involved in de Périgord's murder provoked an outburst that disrupted the pattern of the examination.

'Oh no!' Colbert shouted. 'You are not going to drag me into this sordid affair! How dare you suggest that I was in any way responsible for the death of this disreputable scoundrel, this notorious pervert?' He switched to sarcasm. 'You appear to have forgotten, Monsieur le Juge, that I was still in Africa when the snake was sold. And if I had wished to murder de Périgord, would I have used a snake? Credit me with a little intelligence, please. Snake bites are rarely lethal and as a weapon the bite of a cobra would be particularly inefficient.'

Loubet continued, patient but insistent, questioning Colbert, and ignoring his outburst. Gautier decided he need not listen any longer. Slipping unobtrusively out of the room, he went to collect Surat from the Sûreté and they set out together in a fiacre for Faubourg St Germain. It had been in a new black De Dion-Bouton that the Comte de Chartres had been driven to the Moulin Rouge when he tried to confront Monsieur Windsor. That might be no more than coincidence, for there would be several such models in Paris, but it would be easy to find out if it was.

The door of the Comte's home was opened by a footman, who took Gautier's card and went back into the house, leaving them on the doorstep. Presently, he returned and told them that the Comtesse was not at home. While they had been waiting, Gautier had noticed that a De Dion-Bouton was standing in the courtyard outside the stables and that a chauffeur was washing it. He recognized the chauffeur as the man who had been waiting for the Comte with an automobile outside the Moulin Rouge.

'Perhaps we have not wasted our time coming here after all,' he told Surat, and they crossed the courtyard towards the stables.

The chauffeur looked up as they approached. He was wearing leather breeches, and the long dust coat, cap and goggles which he would put on when driving, hung from a nail on one of the stable doors. Gautier told him who he was, and then added, 'We are here to make enquiries into the death of a man in the 18th *Arrondissement.*'

'What has that to do with me, Inspector?'

'This car was seen standing in a street not far from the murdered man's apartment yesterday morning.'

The chauffeur stared at him uncomprehending but alarmed. 'What are you suggesting?'

'It is very unusual for an expensive automobile to be seen in that *quartier*. Were you the chauffeur?'

'I was driving it, yes.'

'The automobile was stationary when it was seen. Does that mean you were waiting for someone?'

'Yes; for my mistress, the Comtesse.'

At that moment they heard the sound of hurrying footsteps, and looking round saw that the footman had left the house and was running in their direction. 'Monsieur!' he called out. 'Monsieur l'Inspecteur! The Comtesse has returned. She will see you now.'

'I rather thought she might,' Gautier remarked to Surat as they followed the man to the house. The chauffeur was plainly relieved to see them go.

The Comtesse was waiting for them in the drawing-room and one could see that she was displeased. Her anger showed not in her eyes but in lines of discontented petulance around her mouth. She must have been a spoilt and wilful child, Gautier thought.

'You should have asked my permission before speaking to my servants, Inspector.'

Gautier had been right when he thought she might see him through a window of the house speaking to the chauffeur. He said, 'I intended to, Madame, but I was told you were not at home.'

'You were misinformed. The footman did not know I was here.'

'The chauffeur tells me that he drove you to the 18th *Arrondissement* yesterday morning. May I ask what was the purpose of your visit?'

'Really, Inspector! I cannot see why that should be of any interest to the police. If you must know, I went to see one of my pensioners, a man named Victor.'

'Your pensioners, Madame?'

'One of the poor people whom I try to help.'

Gautier knew that many affluent families in Paris had poor people whom they would regularly help by giving them food and old clothes. Usually those who were being helped in this way would call at the homes of their benefactors once a week or sometimes even more often to receive the gifts. He had never heard them described as pensioners, but in a way they were.

'Poor Victor is a former soldier who has fallen on hard times. He has not come to the house for some weeks now and I was worried in case he had fallen ill. So I went to see if he was all right.'

'And was he?'

'I never found him. He must no longer be living there.'

'You were seen leaving the home of a man named Dumas, who is known to the police.'

Alarm flared in the eyes of the Comtesse. She had been lying and was wondering how her lies had been betrayed. The alarm did not last and rapidly she switched to another story.

'I know nothing about that. I knocked on the door of the apartment where I understood Victor lived. No one answered, so I left.'

'You did not try to open the door?'

'I did, of course, but it was locked. Why do you ask?'

'Because soon afterwards the body of a man was found in that apartment. He had been shot in the head.'

'Mother of God! By whom?'

'That is what we are trying to establish.'

The Comtesse stared at Gautier in astonishment. 'My God, surely you do not suspect me of having killed him? At what time was he shot?'

'We believe it must have been sometime late last evening.'

'But you were with me here last evening, Inspector!'

'I am aware of that, Madame.' As he was speaking, Gautier remembered Catriona Becker pointing out that he had been in her apartment when Armand de Périgord was killed. Was it no more than chance that both women could rely on him to prove that they were not present when two murders had been committed? He added, 'And after I left here you had another visitor.'

'What visitor? Who?'

'I was hoping that you would tell me who it was.'

'I had no other visitors. Almost as soon as you left I retired to bed.' The Comtesse could not resist smiling as she added, 'Alone!'

'As I was leaving, I saw a man arriving at your house.'

'Then it must have been a friend of one of my servants.'

Gautier decided it was time for him to go. The murder of Dumas would in due course be the subject of a judicial enquiry and the Comtesse would have to appear before a *juge d'instruction*. By discussing the matter any further, he might inadvertently be coaching her, helping her to prepare answers to what the judge might ask her. He had, nevertheless, one more question to ask her.

'One final question, Madame. How many people beside Madame Becker knew that you were being blackmailed?'

'None.'

'You told no one else?'

'No. I was afraid of what the blackmailer might do if I did.'

Leaving the home of the Comtesse, Gautier and Surat set out for the Ile de la Cité. They walked, because in all probability that day's session before the *juge d'instruction* would be ending soon, if it was not already over. The processes of the law moved at a ponderous speed and members of the Department of Justice could see no reason for expediting them by working long hours.

As they were walking along the banks of the Seine, Surat remarked, 'The Comtesse de Chartres is a beautiful woman, is she not?'

Gautier smiled, remembering the Comtesse's attempt to seduce him the previous night. 'She is, but not a very accomplished liar.'

Chapter 18

An evening at the circus was a favourite entertainment for Parisians of all ages, and the Cirque Alfredi was one of the largest circuses in the city. L'Hippodrome was the oldest and best known, but because of the daring of its performers and the equestrian skills of its lady riders, the Cirque Alfredi was rapidly overtaking it in popularity. Instead of the classic circus ring, it had a rectangular arena more than one hundred and fifty metres in length. This could have been why the American showmen had chosen it to stage their 'Wild West Extravaganza', as it would give more space for the gun battle between cowboys and Red Indians which, according to the posters posted all over Paris, would be the climax of the performance.

Spectators were seated in banked rows of seats, with a low rail separating them from the piste, and behind them were the private boxes, for circuses were no longer the purlieu of ordinary people. Increasingly, the *gratin* and affluent bourgeoisie would take boxes, in which they could entertain their guests, at a comfortable distance from the noise and the sweat of the animals and the performers. At the back of the boxes were the cages and stables where, during the intervals of a performance, the audience were allowed to stroll and gaze at the animals.

That evening when Gautier arrived at the Cirque Alfredi, he was shown to Madame Becker's box by an attendant, who was plainly a Frenchman but who wore the outfit of a cowboy, complete with a wide-brimmed hat, leather chaps, spurs and two revolvers in holsters at his hips. He noticed that all the attendants were dressed in similar fashion which, he supposed, must all be part of American showmanship about which one heard so much.

When Gautier reached the box, he saw that Catriona had not yet arrived but that the Comtesse de Chartres and Marcel Colbert were sitting close together talking. The subject of their conversation appeared to be giving neither of them any pleasure, with Colbert emphasizing everything he said with vehement gestures and the Comtesse plainly uneasy, perhaps even frightened. As Gautier approached, they stopped talking and the Comtesse looked up at him.

'I am comforted to see you arrive, Inspector,' she said.

'Comforted, Madame?'

'Reassured, then. Have you seen the revolvers that the attendants are carrying?'

'I would imagine that they are not loaded.'

Colbert appeared to have lapsed into a sullen silence, and Gautier supposed he might still be resentful of having had to appear before the *juge d'instruction*. He wondered too why Madame Colbert was not at the Cirque Alfredi that evening. Had the evidence of her infidelity with de Périgord led to an irreparable rupture in their marriage, or was Colbert excluding her from social engagements as a punishment?

The conversation between the three of them limped along until Catriona Becker arrived, accompanied by Sigmund Locke and Luc Deslandes. They were brought to the box by another attendant dressed as a cowboy. His face, with its black beard and ample moustaches, seemed familiar to Gautier, but he could not place it. The attendant, too, looked as though he might have recognized Gautier, but he said nothing.

One might have thought that a circus was not a form of entertainment which would appeal to a man as grave as Sigmund Locke, but he must have been at home in Catriona's social circle, for she did not introduce him to her other guests. Instead, she told them where she wanted them to sit. Locke was given the place of honour on her

179

right and the seat on her left was left empty for the Prefect of Police. The Comtesse de Chartres was placed on Locke's right and Gautier sat next to her.

The Prefect had still not arrived when the Wild West Show opened with a grand parade of all the performers, led by a brass band in blue and gold uniforms. The band was far better than any brass band that one would hear in France. The French were as musical as any nation, and French instrumentalists as good as any in the world, but French military bands invariably produced a hideous cacophony of sound. This may have been a reflection of the individuality of the musicians. Not long previously, a Minister of War had been shocked to hear that army bands were playing no less than forty different versions of the national anthem.

Behind the band came the leader of the troupe, a colourful character, mounted on a splendid white horse and carrying a large white hat which he took off and waved to the audience. The applause as the parade passed was polite but without any of the wild enthusiasm which the Americans may have been expecting. The spectators were curious, but not yet convinced that the New World had any spectacles to offer better than those of their own country.

The rest of the performers were mainly cowboys: some on foot, twisting lassos and doing tricks with ropes as they walked, others mounted, firing their revolvers and shouting what one supposed would be their calls to cattle. Behind them came a couple of dozen Red Indians, half-naked and with feathers in their scalps, led by an Indian chief with an imposing head-dress.

As the parade filed past, the Comtesse leant over and said to Gautier, quietly, for the sound of the band and the shooting made whispering superfluous, 'I must see you alone later this evening. There is something important I have to tell you.'

Gautier had an uneasy feeling that the previous night he had narrowly escaped falling into some trap which the Comtesse and the Prefect of Police had planned. He had

180

no wish to risk being trapped again, so he replied, 'If it is important it would be better for you to tell me now.'

'How can I with everyone around?'

'Wait until the first interval and I will invite you to come with me and see the animals. We can talk there.'

After the parade had ended, the show began with a contest between cowboys riding unbroken horses. The horses reared and bucked and the skill of the riders in staying mounted was astonishing. Catriona Becker leant across towards Gautier and said to him in English, 'They call this "bronco busting" in America.'

'So you whisper to each other in English now!' the Comtesse said petulantly.

The show continued with displays of skill with the lasso and of sharp-shooting with rifles. These were followed by more riding, bareback this time, and then by a contest in the roping of steers. The longhorn cattle with their spread of horns may have been not too difficult to rope, but the horns were sharp enough to be dangerous and one cowboy was dragged off his horse by the steer he had roped and gored, receiving an ugly wound in his thigh.

Catriona had ordered champagne for her guests during the first interval in the performance and it was brought by the same attendant who had escorted her, Locke and Deslandes to the box and who appeared to have been designated to look after the party throughout the show. Once again, Gautier had the feeling that he had seen the man before and he noticed that as he served champagne to Locke and Deslandes, he was staring at them intently.

'The Comtesse wishes to look at the horses,' Gautier told Catriona, 'so I will escort her to the stables. We will have our champagne when we return.'

As they were on their way to the stables, he said to the Comtesse, 'Now what is it that you wish to tell me?'

'I have a confession to make. What I told you this afternoon was untrue.'

'About your reason for going to the apartment of the man Dumas?'

'Yes. I was not visiting a pensioner. If I had been, I

181

would certainly not have visited him in that district of Paris.' The fact that she had lied did not appear to embarrass the Comtesse in any way. 'The place was disgusting and in all probability dangerous.'

'Why did you go, then?'

'I was looking for Lucien. As I told you last night, I think he may have copies of the photograph and might use them to continue blackmailing me.'

'What made you go to that particular apartment?'

'I was given that address and told I would find Lucien there. When there was no answer to my knock, I tried the door and found it was not locked. So I looked inside.' The Comtesse shut her eyes as though to shut out the memory of what she had found beyond the door. 'The man Dumas was lying stretched out on the bed dead. His body was quite cold. It was horrible!'

'And you went away leaving him there?' The Comtesse nodded. 'Why did you not tell someone and have the police called?'

'I was terrified! After all, suppose the murderer was still there, hiding in the room. All I could think of was to get away as quickly as possible and to return home.'

'Why did you not tell me this when I came to see your home this afternoon?'

'I did not wish to become involved.'

'Then why are you telling me now?'

'Monsieur Colbert has been telling me of his cross-examination by the *juge d'instruction*. I realize that the murder of Dumas will also be the subject of an official hearing and the magistrate would be merciless to me, if he knew I had lied to you.'

Gautier decided that this time the Comtesse might well be telling the truth, even though her reasons for doing so were far from convincing. As he had told Surat, she was a poor liar and, like many bad liars, she was even more uncomfortable when she was telling the truth. While they had been talking, they had walked the full length of the stable and cages, without even glancing at the horses and cattle which were waiting there. Now they turned and walked back towards the arena.

'Who told you that you would find Lucien at that address?'

'I received an anonymous telephone call,' the Comtesse replied without hesitation. She had been expecting the question and had come with a lie prepared. Gautier knew it was a lie, for an anonymous telephone caller would never reach the Comtesse. She and Catriona Becker and other ladies of the *gratin* were protected by servants who would answer the telephone and insist on knowing a caller's name.

'When was this?'

'Last night; not long after you left, as it happens.'

'Was the caller a man or a woman?'

The question was one which the Comtesse had not expected, but her hesitation was only momentary. 'A man.'

The interval was not over when they reached the private box, but the Prefect of Police had arrived. Taking a glass of champagne from the attendant, Gautier went over to him.

'I have just been apologizing to our hostess,' the Prefect said.

'You warned me that your heavy social programme might take its toll,' Gautier remarked, smiling.

'Social programme? Oh, you mean the opera. That was an ordeal, I can tell you. *Pelléas et Mélisande* by that scoundrel Debussy. It is not a particularly long opera, but last night it seemed to last for ever.'

Soon afterwards, the second part of the show began. To Gautier, many of the acts were similar to those which had gone before, although no doubt there were subtle differences which a connoisseur of Wild West life would have detected. As he was watching, he thought of what the Prefect of Police had said. Was it possible, he wondered, that the Prefect was claiming he had been at the opera the previous evening in case Gautier might have seen him arriving at the Comtesse's house? When he had seen the Comtesse, she would certainly have told him that Gautier had been there and had only just left. She may even have told him of the photograph of herself which was in Gautier's possession.

On reflection, he told himself that his suspicions were absurd. No one would have told such a transparent lie. It would have been too easy to establish whether the Prefect had been at the performance of *Pelléas et Mélisande*. An evening at the opera was a social event in Paris. People went to be seen as much as to watch the performance. Before the opera started, on the great staircase and in the magnificent foyer with its painted ceiling and chandeliers, men in full evening dress and women in evening gowns would stroll, mingle in groups and allow themselves to be admired. He could picture the Prefect, poised and relaxed, among them.

Then the picture in his mind of the opera dissolved and was replaced by another, more vivid. He could see himself, standing in the street opposite the entrance to the home of the Comtesse de Chartres and waiting. He had been glad he was not wearing evening dress, for the white of a shirt front might have attracted the attention of the man who was approaching. Now suddenly he remembered that the man had also not been in evening dress. He could not for that reason have been the Prefect of Police, slipping away after the opera to see his mistress the Comtesse.

Looking past Catriona Becker, Gautier could see the Prefect and beyond him Luc Deslandes. The facial features of the two men were in no way similar, especially since Deslandes had shaved off his beard, but the resemblance in physique, build, the slope of the shoulders and the shape of head now seemed even more pronounced. From that thought, Gautier's brain accelerated, following one idea with another, recalling events and seeing them fall into a pattern. Suddenly he knew what he must do.

Slipping quietly out of his seat he went to the back of the box. The attendant who had brought the champagne was standing there, waiting, he assumed, in case Catriona or her guests might need any further service.

'Are there any police on duty here this evening?' he asked him.

The man blinked, surprised or possibly alarmed at the

question, wondering why the police might be required. 'There are policemen on duty outside the entrance to the circus, Monsieur.'

'But none inside?'

'There may well be. The safety of the spectators and performers is the responsibility of an American company and they would be able to tell you. They have an office just inside the main entrance.'

When Gautier found the office, he saw that a notice with the name THE WILMINGTON DETECTIVE AGENCY was pinned on the door. Inside, two men, both Americans, were making an impressive display of doing nothing. He introduced himself and asked them whether he could find any police officers in the building.

'Is anything wrong, Inspector?' one of the men asked anxiously.

'Nothing that requires police action; not at this stage, anyway. I merely wish to send an important message to my assistant in Paris.'

'In that case, we can help you. We have messengers at our disposal. Just give us the message and tell us where you want it taken.'

Taking a sheet of paper which one of the men gave him, Gautier wrote a message for Surat, with precise instructions on what he wished him to do. Surat was not on duty, but he would not mind being disturbed at home. By then he would have finished his evening meal and, now that his children were adults and spent less time at home, he found the evenings dull. There was nothing to do, he often complained to Gautier, until he could persuade his wife to abandon her embroidery and go to bed. Behind his façade of self-restraint and decorum, Surat was passionately uxorious. Judge Loubet would also not mind being disturbed, for he had told Gautier he would be at home that evening in case there were any new developments in the de Périgord affair. One of the Americans took the message and promised that it would be delivered immediately.

Before he left to return to the arena, on a sudden

impulse Gautier asked the American, 'Does a Frenchman, a Monsieur Montbrun, work for your company by any chance?'

'Theo Montbrun? Yes, he is one of our detectives. Why, do you know him?'

'I know of him, that's all.' Gautier would have liked to ask on what assignment Montbrun was working at that time, but he had always heard that American detective agencies were proud of their codes of ethics and their confidentiality. So he merely thanked the two men and left.

Returning to Catriona's private box, he saw that there was a pause in the performance and that in the arena the scene was being set for what his programme had told him would be the finale of the Wild West Show. The piste was being stripped of fences and hurdles and five-barred gates, and props for the finale were being placed in position. The attendant was still at his station in the box, and when he saw Gautier arrive, he asked him, 'Were you able to find any police, Inspector?'

'No, but it was only a messenger that I needed.'

Instead of taking his seat, Gautier waited at the rear of the box, wondering how he could catch the Prefect's attention. His problem was solved when the Prefect looked round, wondering perhaps where Gautier had gone and why he had been away so long. When he saw Gautier beckon, he came back to join him.

'What is it, Gautier?'

'I would welcome your advice, Monsieur le Préfet, on how to deal with an awkward situation.'

'What situation?'

'I know now who was responsible for the murder of de Périgord.'

'I see. And you wish to leave now so that you can arrest the murderer? Just go, and I will make your excuses to Madame Becker after the show is over.'

'That is not my difficulty, Monsieur. You see, the person I have to arrest is one of Madame Becker's guests.'

'One of the people here this evening? You cannot be serious!'

186

'Unfortunately, it is true.' Gautier did not wish to mention a name. As the performance had not yet restarted, the arena was relatively quiet and he might be heard. So he simply pointed towards Luc Deslandes.

The Prefect stared at him in disbelief. 'Do you have evidence to support your accusation?'

'Yes, but we will need more. I am confident that we can find it. You can see my difficulty, Monsieur. To arrest him now would be a painful embarrassment for Madame Becker.'

'Embarrassment? She would never forgive you! Surely, Gautier, if you insist on making an arrest, you could do it later when the man is at home.'

'I would prefer to do it in the presence of the other guests. Everyone here this evening has in one way or another been associated with de Périgord. In due course, they may all be required to attend the judicial enquiry. It would be better to see their reactions to an arrest now, before they have time to think and rehearse their stories.'

'They will all be shocked.'

'Some may be, but not all of them.'

The final act in the Wild West Show was beginning. From the entrance at one end a stagecoach drawn by four horses moved slowly towards the centre of the arena. Beside the driver of the coach sat a guard, cradling a rifle in his arms. The coach stopped and the passengers, two men and two women, climbed out to stretch their legs. They had scarcely done so when shrill whooping cries were heard and a tribe of Red Indians, some armed with bows and arrows, some with rifles, rode into the arena. The driver of the coach rose in his seat, suddenly clutched at his chest and slowly toppled to the ground. One could see then that by some trick an arrow seemed to be lodged in his breast. The Indians began riding around the coach, whooping and firing, while the guard and then the passengers returned their fire with rifles. Presently, the two men passengers fell dead. Just then a group of cowboys came to the rescue of the coach, riding into the arena with revolvers drawn. They took up their positions around

187

the coach, shooting at the circling Indians. The noise was deafening.

'In that case, Gautier,' the Prefect said, raising his voice to be heard above the noise, 'as we are all going to supper in the private room of a restaurant after the show is ended, why don't you arrest Deslandes then?'

'I will save you gentlemen the trouble,' they heard a man's voice say.

Looking round, they saw that the cowboy attendant was standing behind them and had drawn both his revolvers from their holsters. Startled, the Prefect backed away.

'I will not introduce myself,' the attendant said, smiling.

'You have no need to,' Gautier replied. He knew now why the man's face had seemed familiar. 'You're Lucien, are you not?'

'I should have known you would guess,' Lucien said, 'just as I was confident you would work out who had killed my friend, Armand de Périgord. You have saved me a lot of trouble, Inspector.' He moved away from them and towards the row of seats at the front of the box where the rest of the party were sitting.

'What are you going to do?' the Prefect asked.

'Kill Deslandes of course.' Lucien was still smiling but the hard chill in his eyes was frightening.

'Don't be a fool,' Gautier said, taking a pace forward. 'Give me those revolvers.'

'Don't force me to kill you as well, Inspector.' The noise coming from the arena had abated slightly and, hearing the raised voices, the others in the box looked round. Lucien looked at them and added threateningly, 'Nor any of you.'

'What is this?' Catriona asked.

Instead of answering, Lucien stepped forward and as he reached Deslandes, jabbed one of the revolvers in his shoulder. Deslandes stared at him in disbelief. 'That's right, my friend,' Lucien said. 'Look at me. I would not want you to die without knowing who killed you and why.'

Fear flared in Deslandes's eyes. He leapt to his feet to

face Lucien, and tried to back away. 'Who are you? What do you want?'

'You killed my friend Armand, my lifelong friend and protector. It was you who placed the bomb in his carriage. You might have killed me as well, had I been driving for him that night. A pity you did not, for now I am going to kill you.'

'You're mad! I have no idea what you are talking about!' The fear in Deslandes's eyes was turning to panic. He appealed to Gautier, 'Inspector, who is this madman?'

'The Inspector cannot help you. He was about to arrest you himself for Armand's murder, were you not, Inspector? And now I am going to save him the embarrassment.'

Slowly Lucien raised one of his revolvers till it was pointing at Deslandes. Deslandes lashed out, knocking the barrel of the gun away. Then, twisting, he leapt over the low barrier that separated the private box from the spectators' seats in front. An aisle between the rows of seats ran down to the side of the arena and Deslandes began running down it. Lucien followed him, impeded by his chaps and spurs, jumped the barrier and fired one shot at Deslandes which missed and ricocheted off the back of a seat. The noise of the shot was drowned by the cries of the Indians as the mock battle in the arena raged. When he reached the last row of seats, Deslandes looked round and saw Lucien chasing him, still pointing his revolvers towards him. Recklessly he jumped the rail and began running across the piste, dodging between the horses of the Indians who were still galloping around the marooned stagecoach. He got past one horse, the rider of another swerved and missed him, but the next one collided with him. The horse fell, dislodging its rider as it knocked Deslandes to the ground and rolled on him. The audience, thinking this was a stunt and all part of the act, cheered.

Almost at the same time, the sound of a trumpet was heard, and from the opposite end of the arena a troop of soldiers appeared, galloping to the rescue and led by the leader of the show dressed in the uniform of a colonel.

For a few seconds, the noise of rifle shots was deafening, until at last the Indians turned and fled, galloping out of the other end of the arena to the sound of cheering from the crowd. Then the band began to play and the performers started to line up to take the applause.

Two attendants who were on duty by the side of the piste had seen Deslandes being knocked down. Now they hurried out, picked him up and carried him to the side of the arena. Someone was calling for an ambulance. Catriona and her guests were on their feet, staring in horror at what they had seen.

Chapter 19

The private room in Claudel's restaurant where the supper party was held that evening was expensively elegant, with Louis Quinze furniture, crystal and silver table settings and attentive waiters hovering in the background. Catriona Becker's guests were not in a mood though to appreciate the room's studied elegance. Slow to recover from the shock and horror of the drama they had watched played out at the Cirque Alfredi, they stood holding the aperitifs which the waiters had served them and waiting uneasily.

Catriona had been tempted to cancel the supper, but she knew that two more guests would be joining them at the restaurant. One was the Prefect's wife, who had been unable to attend the Wild West Show as she suffered from a rare complaint which made her allergic to horses. Even for her to pass too close to a horse would bring on a kind of seizure, in which she would choke and find difficulty in breathing. As a result, she spent most of her days in the seclusion of her home and only went out in carriages or automobiles which were virtually hermetically sealed. The other guest was Madame Léontine Colbert, who that day had gone to visit relatives outside of Paris, but would return in time to join the party for supper.

The conversation of the other guests as they waited for the two of them to arrive was stilted. No one wished to remember the sight of Luc Deslandes being carried from the arena and taken to hospital. His neck had been broken and he was not expected to live. Although nobody spoke of it, Gautier realized that everyone was expecting an explanation. Some of them would have heard Deslandes being accused of the murder of de Périgord. Others would be wondering why an attendant at the Wild West Show had tried to shoot him. Gautier also knew that it was he who would have to give the explanation. He was reluctant to begin, for any elucidation must reveal stories which some would not wish to hear; stories of their indiscretions, infidelity and deceit.

Finally, it was Catriona who made it impossible for him to delay any longer. 'Who was it who tried to shoot Luc?' she asked.

'A man named Lucien.'

'Armand de Périgord's servant?' the Prefect asked.

'He was not really a servant. They had been close friends since they were boys.'

'Two *pédés* together, no doubt,' Colbert remarked acidly.

'Possibly. If they were, it is not significant.'

'But why on earth should he have wished to shoot Deslandes?' Sigmund Locke asked. He may have been slightly deaf and had missed what Lucien had shouted at the Wild West Show.

'Did you not hear him?' Catriona explained. 'He said that Luc had murdered Armand.' She looked at Gautier. 'Was that the truth?'

'It was.'

'I refuse to believe it,' the Comtesse de Chartres protested. 'What possible reason could Luc have had for killing Armand?'

'Revenge, no doubt,' the Prefect suggested. 'De Périgord had been responsible for the break-up of his parents' marriage. And therefore indirectly for his father's suicide.'

'And the reason why he was forced to resign his commission,' Colbert added.

'Luc was not violent.' The eyes of the Comtesse were full of tears. 'He was a gentle man. Someone else must have killed Armand and you are blaming Luc because he cannot defend himself.'

192

'Can you suggest who the murderer might be?' the Prefect asked her. 'De Périgord's death must have been convenient for a number of people.'

The sarcasm in his tone did not escape the Comtesse and she flushed. Gautier could understand why the Prefect might wish to remind her of the folly of her behaviour with de Périgord and the trouble it had caused him, but there was a streak of cruelty in his taunt. He had never thought of the Prefect as a cruel man and wondered whether he might be retaliating for some hurt the Comtesse had done him in the past.

'The man was a troublemaker,' Sigmund Locke said. 'I am surprised that someone did not remove him before.'

Locke's tone was not vindictive or even malicious and, for that reason, his remark was more chilling than the Prefect's. One could well imagine that he would have had no hesitation in having de Périgord eliminated and it would have been done more efficiently and more anonymously than with a bomb in a public park. As it was, Luc Deslandes had pre-empted him, saving the embarrassment that his wife's secret forays to de Périgord's hotel room might have caused.

'Few will mourn him,' the Prefect agreed.

'Lucien will,' Catriona said.

After attempting to kill Deslandes and seeing him being knocked down in the arena, Lucien had made no attempt to escape, but had surrendered quietly to the police. He had been taken into custody and would appear before Judge Loubet the next day. He appeared to have accepted whatever fate awaited him with resignation.

'What will happen to Lucien?' Catriona asked Gautier. 'We know he tried to kill Luc, but he did not succeed, did he?'

'He will have to face trial for attempted murder.'

Gautier was going to add that Lucien had also been responsible for the death of Yvette, the chambermaid at the Hôtel Meurice. He had only just begun when he was interrupted by the arrival of the Prefect's wife and Madame Colbert, who were shown into the room by a

193

waiter. The Prefect's wife was a small woman, who, it seemed, was ready to play a passive role in her husband's life. Madame Colbert seemed to be in good spirits, but her cheerfulness crumbled before the look which Colbert gave her.

'You all look very sombre,' the Prefect's wife remarked, looking round the group.

The Prefect tried to break the news gently. 'Luc Deslandes has had a serious accident.'

'An accident?'

'Why not tell them you are accusing him of having murdered Armand?' the Comtesse asked, her voice shrill with bitterness.

The Prefect began recounting what had happened at the Cirque Alfredi. As she listened, Madame Colbert's incredulity turned slowly into horror. Almost a week had passed since de Périgord's death and the grief she must have felt had begun to abate. Now it returned and she began to sob. Her husband looked at her contemptuously. The Prefect's wife remained calm. She would have heard just as distressing stories of violence and crime, many times during her married life.

'Do you have proof that Luc had Armand killed?' Catriona asked Gautier.

'I have no doubt we will find proof enough.'

'Are you saying that he killed this man Dumas as well?' the Comtesse demanded. 'Why should he have?'

'To protect himself,' the Prefect said. 'Dumas made the bomb and planted it in de Périgord's carriage. Luc was afraid he might tell the police.'

'I think we will find that Deslandes made the bomb himself,' Gautier said. 'He served in an artillery regiment, so he would have the skills needed.'

'In that case, why should he have shot Dumas?'

'To divert suspicions from himself. He wanted us to believe that Dumas had been paid to make the bomb. Then we would assume that he had been shot by whoever had paid him.'

As she realized the implications of what Gautier had

said, the Comtesse gasped. Before she could say anything, the Prefect turned to Catriona. 'Forgive me, Madame, but should we not be starting supper soon? I for one am famished.'

Catriona smiled gratefully, for she realized that the Prefect's intervention was timely. 'You are absolutely right, Monsieur. Let us take our seats and we will be served immediately.'

Gautier too was grateful that he had been interrupted. Everyone in the room must be wondering how and how much the Comtesse knew about the death of Dumas. No one had asked the question, but again an answer would be expected and any answer would lead inevitably to a disclosure that de Périgord had been blackmailing the Comtesse and Catriona. Gautier had little sympathy for the Comtesse, who had lied to him and whose difficulties had been caused by her own vanity and stupidity, but he did not wish to embarrass Catriona, nor to put her engagement to Wayne Archer in jeopardy, even though privately he was beginning to think it might be too late for that.

During supper, the party began talking about the Wild West Show, not with any great enthusiasm, but to avoid the painful subject of de Périgord's murder. Colbert said little and gave the impression that his resentment at the indignities he had suffered was still smouldering. Eventually, he could no longer contain his irritation.

'What about this snake in de Périgord's bed?' he demanded. 'I have almost been accused of putting it there. Who did? Luc Deslandes?'

'No. Lucien,' Gautier replied.

'But why should he want to kill his master? Especially if they were such close friends?'

'There was no question of the snake killing de Périgord. He knew it would be in the bed.'

Now, everyone, including the Prefect of Police, was incredulous and they began asking questions. Gautier told them how Lucien, posing as Laborde, had bought the snake from Colbert's assistant, smuggled it into the Hôtel

Meurice and left it in de Périgord's bed. De Périgord was meant to return from his dinner party, find the snake and kill it with one of the swords in the suite. Lucien had probably never stayed in a hotel before and would not have realized that the bedcovers would be turned down by one of the domestic staff.

'But what was the object of this farce?' Colbert asked.

'De Périgord believed his life was in danger. It had become an obsession that someone was trying to kill him. He may well have received threats on his life.'

'Threats? From whom?'

'As Monsieur le Préfet has already said, a number of people may have wished de Périgord dead.'

The uncomfortable silence which followed Gautier's reply showed him that he need not elaborate on it. Two ladies in the room had been blackmailed by de Périgord, a third was having an affair with him and her husband may well have been aware of it. Even Sigmund Locke might have wished to silence de Périgord to protect his wife. Nor should one ignore the possibility that de Périgord may have been involved in selling secrets to a foreign power.

'But could this masquerade with the snake protect his life?' Catriona asked.

'As you once said of me,' Gautier replied, restraining a smile, 'de Périgord was too clever by half. He thought that if it were shown that his life was in danger, the police would give him protection. After all, he was doing secret work for the Government.'

'But the plan did not work, did it?'

'Up to a point it did. We gave him police protection for a time.'

'What? Are you saying it was withdrawn?' the Comtesse asked indignantly.

'The police cannot give anyone protection for ever.' As he replied, Gautier was conscious that it was not the first time he had made excuses for Courtrand. 'And, rightly as it happens, we were not even certain that the snake had been intended to kill de Périgord.'

'The decision to withdraw the protection was not Inspector Gautier's,' the Prefect said.

'I suggest we stop talking about this dreadful business,' Catriona said. She may have been afraid that any prolonged conversation about de Périgord would come dangerously close to the subject of blackmail. 'Then we can enjoy our supper.'

'I agree,' Madame Colbert said unexpectedly.

'And so do I,' the Prefect said. 'We'll be weary of it soon enough. All Paris will be talking of nothing else for days.'

The switch in the conversation to more mundane matters was forced at first, but before long everyone was immersed in those subjects which were the daily preoccupation of the *gratin* in Paris: the latest gaffe of the President of the Republic; the automobile race from Nice to Paris, during which speeds of more than one hundred and fifty kilometres per hour were reached; the precious gestures of the aristocratic aesthete Comte Robert de Montesquieu, and the scandalous liaisons of the actress Louisa de Mornand. Gautier listened, divided between admiration for the resilience of Catriona's friends and cynicism for the triviality of their lives.

Not until after midnight did the supper party end. The ladies went to fetch their stoles or wraps and to take precautions against the night air, to which their skins would presently be exposed. The men stayed in the dining-room, finishing their cigars. Earlier in the evening, a waiter had brought a letter for Gautier, which had been delivered by hand and which he had put in his pocket. Now he took it out and saw that it was signed by Judge Loubet. Attached to the letter was the judge's visiting card, on the back of which he had scribbled:

Gautier,

This is the authorization which your assistant Surat asked me to let you have. You did not give your reasons for requesting it, but I am confident that as

197

always they are valid. Please be circumspect in how you handle your search of the house. The family to which it belongs are one of the highest-standing and remember too the distress it has suffered.

Loubet

Sigmund Locke was talking intently to Colbert, sounding him out on possible prospects for capital investment in Africa, so Gautier was able to take the Prefect to one side and show him the letter.

'While we were at the Cirque Alfredi I sent a message to Judge Loubet,' he explained, 'asking him for authorization to search Luc Deslandes's quarters in his mother's house. I had in mind that we would be arresting him this evening and that his rooms must be searched as soon as possible afterwards, for evidence that he had made the bomb which killed de Périgord.'

The Prefect looked worried. 'Surely you will delay the search now?'

'Of course.'

Immediately after Luc had been knocked down, the Prefect himself had telephoned Madame Deslandes, telling her what had happened and giving the name of the hospital to which he was being taken. There would be time enough to search for evidence to prove him guilty when they knew if he was going to live.

'When did you decide that it must have been Deslandes who killed de Périgord?' the Prefect asked.

'Not until I realized that the Comtesse de Chartres had been lying for him. Early this morning the Comtesse went to Dumas's home, because she had been told she would find Lucien there. But when I was with her late last night, she had no idea where Lucien might be found. Soon after I left, Luc Deslandes went to her home. It can only have been he who told her, but this afternoon when I asked her, she said she had heard through an anonymous message. She must have guessed that Luc had shot Dumas and was lying to protect him.'

198

'But if you had worked that out why did you not arrest Deslandes earlier?'

Gautier knew he would have to be frank. He smiled and said, 'Last night as I was leaving the Comtesse's home, I saw a man arrive, but in the darkness I failed to recognize him. I thought it might be you, Monsieur le Préfet.'

For a moment, the Prefect stared at Gautier, astonished and indignant. The indignation was replaced by amusement. 'There is a resemblance between us, I know, for other people have commented on it.' He laughed, and then added, 'A few years ago it might well have been me arriving at her home late at night.'

'You mean—?'

'Yes. She and I were the closest of friends. In fact, I flatter myself that I preceded the Prince of Wales by at least two years.' He grinned. 'To be followed by royalty is quite a compliment, don't you agree, Gautier?'

'I am still bewildered,' Catriona complained to Gautier, 'everything happened so swiftly. When Luc was injured I felt sick. And now I keep imagining I hear the snap as his neck was broken.'

In spite of her efforts, the supper party had ended on a melancholy note, and the guests had dispersed with no more than the conventional courtesies, as though glad the evening had ended. Catriona and Gautier were being driven in her carriage to Boulevard Haussmann, where she said the coachman would leave her, before taking Gautier to his apartment on the Left Bank. Locke was returning to the Ritz, while the Prefect had arranged for a closed automobile to take himself, his wife and the Colberts home.

'Like Maria, I find it hard to believe that Luc Deslandes could have committed such a callous crime, or rather two crimes,' Catriona continued. 'He was her lover, you know.'

'I guessed as much. And, even though she denied it to me, she had also told him that she was being blackmailed.'

'How do you know that?'

199

'Why else would he have told her where she could find Lucien? The Comtesse was afraid that Lucien might have more of the nude photographs. But even before that, Luc had persuaded his mother to come and tell me that you and the Comtesse had conspired to have de Périgord killed.'

'Us? That's absurd! Did he think you would believe such a story?'

'Probably not, but he thought that as soon as the Sûreté looked into the matter, we would find out that de Périgord was blackmailing the two of you.'

'But you already knew!'

'Yes, but Luc was not aware of that. His mother's accusations also gave him an excuse to come and see me. His pretext was to tell me not to believe her, but really it was a fishing expedition. He wished to know whether we were making enquiries to establish who might have made the bomb that killed de Périgord. He found out that we were.'

That, Gautier told Catriona, gave Deslandes the idea of using Dumas to divert attention from himself. With his record, Dumas was an obvious suspect. Deslandes would have known of him and that he had blown up an army barracks. So he met up with him, took him out, made him drunk and murdered him.

'The poor man, how dreadful!' Catriona sighed. 'Well, it's all over now. Wayne will be back soon. We will be married and I can forget this whole foolish chapter of my life.'

'Let us hope so.' Gautier did not tell her he was not as optimistic as she was.

They were travelling along Boulevard Haussmann now and approaching Catriona's apartment. She looked at Gautier. 'Jean-Paul, will you come in for a little while?'

'It is very late, is it not?'

'Yes, but come in just for a few minutes and we can talk. You can help me to calm my nerves and forget this terrible evening. Please!'

'Very well.'

The Scottish maid let them into the apartment and took

Gautier's hat and coat. When Catriona told her she could go to bed, she pointed to a telegram which had arrived earlier in the evening and which lay in a tray on a table inside the front door. As soon as he saw it, Gautier had a presentiment that the telegram held unwelcome news, but Catriona picked it up nonchalantly and they went into the drawing-room together. A decanter of whisky and two glasses waited there and Catriona went towards them.

'Let me pour you a whisky. A "wee dram", as we say in Scotland.'

'Should you not read your telegram first?'

'I am sure it is of no consequence, but I suppose I should.'

The effect on Catriona as she began reading the telegram told Gautier that he had been right. She turned white, shut her eyes for a moment and then began to tremble. He thought for a moment that she was having some kind of seizure and quickly poured her a whisky. Then, without speaking, she handed the telegram to him. The message was from a firm of solicitors in Pittsburgh. It was in English, but Gautier could understand the gist of it.

Their client, Mr Wayne Archer Junior, the solicitors said, had been receiving reports from a detective agency on the conduct of Mrs Catriona Becker during Mr Archer's absence from Paris, France. These reports showed that Mrs Becker had been behaving in a manner totally incompatible with the standards which Mr Archer and his family had always set themselves. In the circumstances, Mr Archer had decided that Mrs Becker would not be a suitable wife for him and any promises that he might have made in this respect were consequently revoked. Mr Archer would not be returning to France and had no wish to communicate with Mrs Becker again.

Catriona looked at Gautier. 'You knew about this, did you not?'

'I guessed that you were being followed by a private detective, yes.'

'Then why didn't you tell me?' Her voice was cold with rage.

'It was only this evening that I realized the detective was following you, not de Périgord.'

She began swearing at him, using epithets which slid from the vulgar to the obscene. Suddenly she threw the whisky in his face, slapped him across the cheek and began hitting him violently with her clenched fists. Gautier tried at first to ward off the blows and then in desperation grabbed her, pinning her arms to her sides. She struggled for a while, still swearing, and then began to sob.

He held her to him, awkwardly, trying to comfort her, and slowly the violence of the sobs began to diminish. She looked up at him, trying to smile, and he thought she was going to stammer an apology for losing her self-control. Instead, she reached up, pulled his face down to hers, and kissed him hard on the mouth.

'Take me to bed.' Her voice was hard and imperious.

'First you abuse me, now you tease me,' Gautier replied lightly.

'I'm serious. Take me to bed.'

'That will solve nothing.'

'You owe it to me.'

She kept on kissing him, pushing his hand away when he tried to check her, forcing his mouth open, biting his lips. He knew then that she was serious, determined that they would make love, and he felt his resistance weakening. She slid her hands inside his coat, drawing his body close to hers. Presently she looked at him and smiled, knowing that he had surrendered.

'Come,' she said, and taking his hand pulled him from the room and down a corridor to her bedroom.

Later, Gautier could remember what followed only indistinctly. She made love with an intensity which surprised him, for he had not believed that the Scots were a passionate race, and as she did, she began crying again. Her breath was warm and so were the tears which coursed down his cheeks and throat and back on to her breasts. He remembered being astonished at her body and at how

202

small it was, small but beautifully proportioned, with tiny breasts, a girl's stomach, firm but smooth, responsive thighs. Then the final moment of ecstasy was over and they lay back, side by side.

After an age of silence she said, 'You know, I feel sorry for Luc Deslandes.'

'You need not be. He has no pity himself, and no scruples. He was ready to betray the Comtesse.'

'Are you not being rather severe?'

'I don't think so. He tricked her into going to find Dumas's body. He knew she would be seen at his apartment and suspected of complicity in his death. Do you know she went there, expensively dressed and in an automobile which she left standing in the street? An automobile, if you please, in that *quartier!*'

'If she was naïve, then so have I been. We were both manipulated by Armand.' Catriona sighed. 'At home we have a children's book called *Alice in Wonderland* about a small girl who finds herself in a fantasy world. I know now that for years I have been living in a fantasy world; a world of princesses and countesses and American millionaires. And, like Alice, I am awakening to reality.'

Gautier understood what she meant. The fantasy figures of her world had shown that they were no more than pasteboard. Beneath its upper crust, the expensive dish '*au gratin*' on which she had been dining was proving disappointingly tasteless. He knew that the best advice he could give Catriona was to go back to Scotland, to leave the intrigue and deceit of a pasteboard world, to live among her own folk and rediscover the values of her childhood.

Turning on one side and propping herself on an elbow, Catriona stroked his cheek with one hand. 'But now I have you, everything will be different.'

Her readiness to assume that, because they had made love he now belonged to her, would have seemed arrogant in any other woman, but Gautier found it oddly moving. He knew that he should warn her of the impermanence of their new relationship; that she had moved into the

203

vacuum created in his life by the departure of Claire Ryan and that other women would follow her. He knew she was vulnerable and he should warn her, but he could not find the words.

Catriona may have sensed what he was thinking, for briefly he could see uncertainty in her eyes. 'You will be mine now, will you not, my love?' she asked.

Before Gautier could reply, assurance returned. 'Now I can really teach you English. Everyone knows that the only way to learn a language is on the pillow.'

'*Chérie*, let us not move too fast,' he began.

She slid one leg over him and then sat up till she was astride him. Her smile as she looked down on him was mocking and triumphant.

'The first lesson in any language is the value of silence. As we say in English, actions speak louder than words. Let me show you what I mean.'